Published in Great Britain by
L.R. Price Publications Ltd, 2021
27 Old Gloucester Street,
London, WC1N 3AX
www.lrpricepublications.com

Cover artwork by L.R. Price Publications Ltd
Copyright © 2021

Used under exclusive and unlimited licence by
L.R. Price Publications Ltd.
James Nash Copyright © 2021

The right of The Author to be identified as author of this work has been asserted in accordance with sections 77 and 78 of the Copyright, Designs and Patents Act, 1988.

ISBN-13: 9781838061067

1537 CONSPIRACY

James Nash

Dedication

The author would like to dedicate this book…

…to family ties, both nearby and across the waters, to friends who read my book and gave me constructive criticism, and to my wonderful wife, who shared in the research of my work – thank you for all your support and encouragement.

…to L.R. Price Publications, who gave me a chance to achieve a lifetime ambition.

Prologue

It all began two years ago, on a quiet Sunday morning in July, with a call from my cousin Roberto.

"Hello, Nathan. I hope it is not too early over there, but I wanted to let you know as soon as I could. I am sorry to be calling you with bad news; our good friend and neighbour Agostino passed away yesterday."

"I didn't even know that he was unwell," I replied, and went on to ask: "How? What did he die of?"

Roberto explained in broken English that nobody yet knew, and that there would be an autopsy, due to the suspicious circumstances in which they found him. Roberto then decided it best to let me digest the news, and said that he would call me back later that day.

Roberto was calling from Terranuova in Italy, where he had resided all his life, in a secluded villa on the outskirts of a beautiful village – the same village my mother was born in, and perhaps there would have remained, had she not met and fallen in love with an English soldier who was stationed nearby.

Terranuova was the perfect place to set up home and raise a family, so after marrying in the romantic city of Venice, my parents settled there and had three children: two girls, followed years later by a son – that would be me. My grandmother on my mother's side and the extended family all lived close by, so we were surrounded by love and security in this village, which I hold so dear to my heart. However, Terranuova may have been a great place to raise children, but there were not many opportunities for the next generation. And so my parents took the agonizing decision to return to England, in the mindset that it would provide us children with better prospects for our future. Dad knew life would be difficult for his Italian wife back in England, as her English was very limited, not to mention the close family ties she would be leaving behind, but he felt still it was for the best.

My mind was now reminiscing, remembering the fun times I'd had back in Italy, and saddened that another large part of my history had passed away: my friend Agostino.

As promised, Roberto called back later that afternoon.

"Hi. Are you okay?" I answered.

Roberto replied: "Yes, I'm okay. Nathan, as you know, we normally bury our dead within a few days, but due to the suspicious circumstances of our friend's death, this will not be happening until they have carried out all their tests. Before calling you this morning I rang to let Agostino's daughter Rosa know about her father, and after my call to you she called me back. Rosa asked if I could keep her informed with news on what happened to her father, and to let me know that she wants to come over for the funeral, then go back home to France as soon as possible. Nathan, she wanted to know if you were still interested in purchasing her father's house, as she had no intentions on returning to Italy to live."

Without hesitation, I replied: "Yes, of course I'm still interested."

"Okay, I will let her know. Speak soon, Nathan." And, with that, Roberto hung up.

Wow! What a difference a day makes!

I poured a large glass of Jack Daniel's and toasted my friend Agostino. He was the village blacksmith and a good friend of the family. Although his daughter was a few years older than me, we often played together with my cousins, sisters and other children in the village. His house held unforgettable memories for me; it was in the old man's home – whom I came to call "Nono", Italian for "Grandad" – that we spent countless hours listening to tales of mythology and village traditions, from this mystifying and larger than life man. I raise my glass and salute you, Agostino.

I tried to relax, and soon found myself reflecting on my life.

My name is Nathan Doyle. At forty-two years old, I had never been married, although I came close on more than one occasion; no offspring, as far as I was aware, and nothing in the present to suggest those things were going to change in the near future. My friends often joked how I must be "nailing it" with the ladies, adding: "How could the ladies resist those big brown eyes and black hair?"

"Thanks, Mum. At least I inherited your looks!" would be my response.

I was part owner of a successful business, owning my own property and a reasonably good company; one would think I was a pretty good catch. So, where was I going wrong? Had I let the girl of my dreams slip away, or had the right one just not come along?

My life in Brighton was tedious, and apart from my business – a small building company – there was nothing that was willing me to stay. My last relationship was a thing of the past and my social life was non-existent.

I reached for the laptop, sat comfortably on my old and very well used leather sofa, and began to search for flights to Pisa airport. I found a vacant seat leaving from Gatwick to Pisa early the following morning, and with one click of a button my reservation was confirmed. The adrenalin started to hit me, as I began to throw a few items of clothing and the necessary toiletries into a travel bag.

The next morning, I left my Victorian home, its style quite typical of the property in this area, and walked speedily toward the station, leaving the buzzing town of Brighton, its pavements littered with the remnants and mayhem of the night before: the odd shoe tossed in the gutter, the discarded takeaway drink cartons, and a ginger tom sitting patiently on the doorstep, waiting for his owner to open the door and let him in.

The journey to the airport was tiresome. It was a hot, humid day and the train was overcrowded, with the majority commuters on their way to work, looking very important as they talked far too loudly on their mobile phones.

Chapter 1

Before boarding, I called my business partner Danny to confirm he had received the message I left on his answering machine, explaining my unexpected departure to Italy.

"Take as much time as you need, mate. The business will still be here when you return." I knew Danny would be able to manage alright without me for a while. We both brought the same skills and passion for building to the business, knowing that either one of us could manage if the other needed time away.

I headed for the departure lounge and, with over an hour before boarding, got myself a bite to eat and a large mug of coffee.

I met Danny when we both applied to join a local building company as apprentices; there were at least thirty candidates and Danny and I were offered the two positions. I learned quickly, and enjoyed the fact that I was able to transform shattered and broken objects into articles of beauty, which in turn could begin life again. My greatest satisfaction was restoring and refurbishing desolated buildings, which had long since lost their splendour.

From a very young age I was interested in antiques; I remember being captivated by their beauty and robustness to survive years gone by. My fascination with this subject enticed me to learn more, and I spent many nights falling asleep whilst perusing books on the delights of 17th-century antiques.

On reflection, the only part of my life thriving was the business. The workload was plentiful, and within a year of opening we had recruited twelve staff to meet the company's deadlines and schedules. The business meant working long hours and took priority in my life. Don't misunderstand me, the work provided me with a good lifestyle, but this came at a price.

My memories drifted back to childhood, playing with my cousins, siblings and Agostino's daughter. Returning to Terranuova for our family reunion was a yearly event, and one which I carried on undertaking after my parents passed away. The sense of belonging – the closeness – never diminished from year to year; they were part of me.

Now, my return was to share in an old friend's departure.

On board the plane, I was seated next to a rather large man with what can only be described as a perspiration problem; just my luck, I thought. Shuffling myself into a reasonably comfortable position, I closed my eyes and drifted off into a deep sleep. Sadly, this was short-lived, as I was woken by the weight of my fellow passenger's head on my shoulder, and the gurgling sounds coming out of his mouth when inhaling and exhaling. Thankfully, the journey to Pisa is a short one, and no sooner were the seatbelt signs turned off than I made my way to the front of the aircraft.

My motion was that of a man on the run, through customs and via airport control. With no baggage to collect, I headed straight to the car-hire counter and took charge of a silver Fiat.

Anxious to arrive before sundown, I hit the accelerator, tuned into a local radio station and set off on my two-hour journey through scenic hillsides and dust-blown farmland, before reaching my destination.

Unknown to me, this was to become the biggest turning point of my life – a journey which would lead to a part of history being discovered, which some would have preferred remained unknown.

I took the turning for Terranuova Bracciolini and meandered my way through the narrow, winding streets to the piazza, the heart of the village.

There was hardly any sign of life; the blazing sun was at its strongest and all inhabitants were securely behind windows heavily guarded with green or brown arched shutters, to keep the heat of the day at bay. The farmacia had closed for lunch, its heavy, grey, metallic shutters locked shut. The newsstand, with its billboards advertising the latest items of gossip, leaning carelessly against windows overcrowded with garish magazines, was also closed. The church, although magnificent in its day, now looked slightly jaded and in need of a coat of paint; still, it stood proudly with the heavy, oak-panelled doors slightly ajar, beckoning inhabitants of the village into the cool of its marbled interior. The fountain, diminutive and lacking any sign of activity, stood somewhat off-centre, on its slightly raised paving slabs.

Roberto's villa stood on the outskirts of the village, significantly superior with its black, wrought-iron gates and walnut double doors, decorated with a gigantic lion's head for a knocker. He was leaning against the trunk of an olive tree, his face slightly hidden by the leafy branches, enjoying the shade the tree provided for the time of day. He greeted me with a bear hug and a friendly slap on the back. His grey steel eyes shone as he grinned, exposing his tobacco-stained teeth, which appeared beneath an exaggerated silver moustache. His unruly mop of ebony hair, silver at the temples, fell over his eyebrows, threatening to block out his vision. There was no doubt that Roberto had aged since the last time I saw him, but even with the signs of maturity he still was a good-looking man.

Within seconds I was surrounded by a horde of shrieking, excited family members, all wanting to welcome me with hugs and kisses. The thunderous, deafening greetings, back-slapping and tugging at my clothing, by those too short to reach higher than my waist, seemed to go on for ages. It was a joyous moment; it felt heartwarming to be amongst family again.

Aunt Marie edged her way through the mass and embraced me to the point of suffocation, with her fleshy arms flung around my chest in a motherly grip. She was the matriarch figure of the family, with empathic, dark eyes, and raven and silver curls falling around her plump face, as well as an ample bosom upon which to rest one's head when in need of comforting. After disentangling myself from Aunt's clutches I gave Uncle Italo, my mother's younger brother, a hug, and followed him to the dining room, where there was a feast fit for a king, which must have taken my aunt all morning to prepare. I felt like a prodigal son coming home to a hero's welcome.

The huge wooden table was adorned with an array of dishes: steaming mushrooms marinated in garlic sauce, tagliatelle, bistecca alla Fiorentina, homemade bread, salad drizzled with Italian olive oil, cheeses and dips of every description, and a fruit basket overflowing with home-grown peaches, grapes, figs and nectarines. The aroma of garlic and the fragrance of freshly baked bread were too much to resist; I dipped a piece of bread in the oil-vinaigrette and washed it down with a generous glass of Montepulciano vino, whilst taking in the atmosphere of happy chatter and feeling a total sense of belonging.

Four hours had passed since arriving at Roberto's villa, and after indulging with another glass of vino and feeling slightly heady, I asked if I could be excused. Although the night was still young, it had been a long day.

I was shown to my room, where I could still hear the whispering sounds of family members coming through the adjoining walls. The bed was a black, wrought-iron four-poster, with a heavily embroidered throw and matching frilled pillowcases. I removed and folded the throw, and put it away in the wardrobe; a sheet was all that was required in this heat. The desire to sleep was overwhelming, contributed to by the journey, the sumptuous meal, the vino and the emotions running through my mind. Moments later, I drifted into a relaxed and deep sleep.

*

The next morning, I awoke to thin rays of sunlight piercing through the wooden slats of the window. There were sounds of children playing, adults talking and the rattling of china coming from the kitchen. It was amusing to wake up to so much activity, and I looked forward to joining them.

Breakfast consisted of an array of Italian biscuits and cakes – and espresso coffee, of course.

"Nathan, shall we go for a walk?"

I nodded in assent, and Roberto and I walked along the overgrown fields which led to the main square.

"The coroner called this morning, to say that he can only come to the conclusion that the old boy died of natural causes, as he could not find any evidence of foul play," Roberto explained. "So, in theory, our friend can be buried tomorrow. But Rosa has asked if we can delay this by a day, so that you can meet with her appointed estate agent at her father's property, to discuss the sale.

Rosa prefers the business side to be sorted before arriving for her father's send-off, as she would prefer to leave straight after."

There followed a short silence, before Roberto continued: "I'm glad you were able to make it for his send-off, Nathan; I know how much he meant to you."

Although my mind was elsewhere, I knew there was much to organize in order to purchase the old man's house. It was no surprise to my family that Agostino's property, which I had admired from a very young age, still held an unexplainable fascination for me – perhaps because of the numerous fond memories I had and the lessons I learned from this incredible person. Becoming the proud owner would be a constant reminder of the man I came to call my Nono.

Aunt Marie and Uncle Italo often spoke of the steep history which surrounded old Agostino's house. According to legend, it used to be a monastery, dating back to the 13th century. During the ninety years that Agostino had been in residence, and whilst certain renovations were being carried out to the adjoining building, builders had discovered a collection of faded frescos, the durable method of wall painting, requiring the use of watercolours on wet plaster. Upon investigation, these paintings were dated as far back as the 7th century, and needless to say all building works were halted. In keeping with the village decor, the old stonework of the building was rendered, painted pale ochre and adorned with wooden shutters.

I stepped into the cool interior and a familiar odour permeated throughout the building, slightly musty but not unpleasant. The stone staircase, worn through age, dipped in the middle. On the ground floor was an area known in Italy as the cantina, which had so many different uses; Agostino used it as a laundry room, and to store whatever he didn't need in the house. I climbed the winding flight of steps steadily, acclimatizing my eyes to the dim, inadequately lit hallway. Roberto's footsteps clattered behind me, echoing our arrival.

We were met by two well-dressed men, with briefcases and documents relating to the property, who shook our hand whilst continuing to converse on their mobiles, presumably to other clients. One of the gentlemen clasped a hand over the receiver, allowing him to relay a gesture for us to look around at our leisure, adding that he would catch up with us en route.

Eager to begin negotiations, I forged ahead into Agostino's old home; I knew the layout well enough, without the aid of the suited bods having to explain any details, and welcomed the opportunity to roam without an escort. Roberto was hot on my heels, breathing heavily from ascending the flight of stairs so rapidly. I went from room to room, savouring each and every moment, and recapturing memories of dashing around this extensive dwelling.

By now, the paintwork was cracked and chipped. Huge chunks of plaster had parted company with the stone walls, leaving crevices the size of a fist. The stone floors lay bare, with no rugs or carpeting, and were worn smooth, cold and clammy. I knew without doubt that the most extraordinary room for me was where Agostino had once slept. It was the only room with the original wooden floor; I always sensed an inner calmness here, and I saved it until last.

The old man's bedroom had no trappings of modern day and was starkly furnished, occupied by only a single bed with a tall, wrought-iron headboard, a small, water-stained side table and a small double-door wardrobe, containing a handful of empty hangers.

I turned slowly and gazed at the opposing wall – and there in front of me was the secret door!

It was no more than a foot in height and width, with an arched, solid walnut door and heavy steel braces. The door remained locked, as always, and brought back the image of the huge iron key I used to see attached to old Agostino's belt which, no doubt in my mind, belonged to this secret door. Agostino, as most Italians, never locked any doors in his home, so it had always intrigued me as to the reason why this one door would be permanently locked, and the key kept so guarded. I had never seen inside this secret door, and looked forward to finally unravelling its secrets!

The condition of the property was irrelevant; the work needed to be undertaken was only cosmetic, and I would enjoy the challenge of restoring this antiquated property to its former glory.

I announced to the bemused, suited bods, their clipboards and biros twitching, that I would be placing an offer, and could they please arrange the necessary meeting with the local notary. Roberto did not say a word; he knew my character well enough to know that determination was one of my strong points, that if my mind was set on something, no stone would remain unturned in order for me to obtain my objective; he knew the late Augustine's property would be mine.

One of the guys looked at me bewildered and said: "I don't think you have understood, Signor Doyle. We are the representatives of the local notary; our instructions are to value the property for tax purposes, and as requested in our client's will, to offer the premises to you at fifty per cent less than its total value."

I stood silently in shock, and felt the love Agostino had demonstrated for me.

Once paperwork was completed, I called Rosa, who had come over from France early today and was staying with family nearby, for her father's funeral tomorrow. Firstly I offered my condolences, then I let her know that the paperwork was being sent to her solicitors as we spoke, and hopefully the sale should be completed in the next four to six weeks.

On the journey back, Roberto shared how happy he was that Agostino's property was "staying in the family", and not being sold to a stranger. There was a long pause then, as if we both wanted a moment to reflect on the enormous void Agostino was leaving.

I broke the silence: "I'm relieved to hear that our friend died of natural causes."

But Roberto was not so sure. "Nathan, two days before his death, Agostino asked me to come over, as he wanted to discuss something with me. I popped over to his house and asked if everything was okay, he poured us both a cup of coffee and told me: 'Roberto, I think I am being followed and I believe somebody has been inside my house. Nothing is missing, but I think what I found hidden in the tabernacle is what they are looking for.' The old boy looked very serious, and continued to tell me that he had found a cross made from gold and encrusted with precious stones, mainly diamonds. It featured an inscription which he could not read, he thought possibly written in Latin.

"Knowing Agostino's character, I was more than skeptical that this was another one of the old man's famous exaggerated stories. But this time, Nathan, I think he was telling me the truth!"

I laughed and said: "Come on, Roberto. The old boy was famous for spinning a good yarn!"

Roberto shook his head; "Nathan, I think this time it was not a story, because he looked very frightened. He went on to tell me: 'I think my big mouth has led them to me.' He then explained that, after discovering the golden cross, he visited his local tavern and was telling his companions about his find. He said some people laughed and praised him on his fascinating story, but he wondered if someone there had innocently repeated his claim to people who knew that this was not a story, but a fact."

I shrugged my shoulders, and hoped that this was not the case.

The next day, family and friends attended in their droves to pay their respects to the man, who was loved by all who knew him.

I thought of mine and Roberto's conversation, and started to feel a shiver down my spine. What if he was murdered? What if there were undiscovered assets hidden in what Agostino referred to as "the secret door"?

Alas, my visit to Italy had to be cut short: so much to organize; money transfers for the deposit to secure the deal; remaining balance to be ready to deposit with Rosa's solicitors, within three weeks of the agreed date; confirmation and signatures for legalities which needed obtaining under Italian law… No prolonging and agonizing, whilst solicitors dragged their heels to ensure higher fees.

After the funeral I bid Roberto, Aunt Marie, Uncle Italo and other relatives farewell, collected my few belongings and headed to Pisa airport, for my return journey back to Brighton.

The journey was non-eventful, but once again the adrenalin started to kick in. My head was buzzing with ideas, knowing this time that I was returning to Brighton purely to put my affairs in order before coming back to Italy. Had I just decided that Italy was going to be my permanent home? All I could think about was returning to Terranuova, and what the next chapter in my life would have in store.

Before this could happen, I knew I had umpteen phone calls to make, and numerous discussions to be had with various people, including my friend and business partner, Danny.

By the time I got home it was late, and after a quick shower and a bite to eat, I jotted a list of things to do in the morning, before heading to bed, to try to get some much-needed sleep.

As soon as the banks, estate agents, solicitors and every other establishment were open, I started the multitude of telephone calls to set my plans in motion.

Hours later, after a frantic succession of moving money between accounts, arranging appointments with the bank manager, solicitor and insurance company, my thoughts drifted to the business I shared with my long-term friend – the business which had kept me sane over the years, not to mention providing me with a significant lifestyle.

Danny Walters and I had worked together for just over ten years and I trusted him with my life. A big, beefy, no-nonsense sort of guy, I knew that Danny would be able to oversee the business for the foreseeable future. Fortunately, there was enough work already booked in to keep the company afloat, and provide both of us with good cash flow. For me, this gave me the opportunity to begin work on my new home in Italy, and for Danny security and time to secure new work for times ahead.

I started making a list of all the materials needed for the renovation, and contacted suppliers to arrange delivery of certain items which I knew would prove difficult to obtain in Terranuova.

I then met Danny at our favourite restaurant on the Brighton marina. We exchanged updates, which led to us talking about the business and the reality of me becoming an overseas partner for a while.

"It will work. I will email you with daily updates. Anyway, you're only a phone call or a plane ride away if absolutely necessary." Danny's reassurance was all I needed.

After several days and sleepless nights, everything needing to be done was done, and everyone needing to be spoken to had been. So, with a last glance around my home, I locked up securely and waited for Danny to pick me up; he insisted on taking me to the airport himself.

The journey was quiet, with only the sound of the radio hazily playing in the background. Deep in thought, conversation was slight; we knew each other well enough to know that there was no need for idle chatter, or demonstrative mention of what our friendship meant to both of us. I was going to miss my old buddy.

Airports during peak holiday season are not good places to be; mayhem reigns and brains are frazzled; irritation comes easily. To overcome the havoc caused by relentless whining little monsters and their over-indulgent parents, I waited for the board to confirm which gate I needed to proceed to from a stool in the bar lounge, nursing a single shot of J.D. swirling in a large quantity of ice cubes. With every sip, my thoughts were immersed in life in Italy; my expectations and anticipation ran riot.

I wished the next few hours away, and after a second J.D. and ice I boarded the plane in a robotic fashion, settling into my allocated window seat. The air hostess greeted the passengers with a familiar welcoming smile, offering a copy of *The Times* newspaper. I took one, to lose myself in something other than me, which turned out very refreshing.

The aircraft took off at full throttle. As we levelled off, high above the clouds, my thoughts returned to the adventure ahead of me, a reality which, up to now, I had only dreamt about. I yearned for the tranquil life I associated with my mother's homeland, and the prospect of living a slower-paced lifestyle; a life without the frustrations of deadlines, or the exasperation of dealing with at least one moron a month, who was hellbent on getting something for nothing, by complaining that the colours or styles – which, I hasten to add, were chosen solely by themselves – were not quite the look they were expecting. Was this now going to become my reality? I closed my eyes and dared to envision it!

The plane touched down at Pisa airport on time.

Ignoring the sign reading *"Do not unfasten your seatbelt until the plane comes to a complete stop,"* I was poised, ready to dodge through the crowds, to march through the long and winding corridors, before queuing once more for a passport control clerk, who was looking at one passport mugshot after another which barely resembled the person standing in front of them. I then stood idly at the baggage carousel, waiting for my luggage, which was adorned with ribbons, just like my mother showed me; Mother would say: "Always tie a few colourful ribbons, so you can easily recognize your luggage."

Roberto was waiting for me at the far end of the barrier. Typical of his jovial character, he was holding a board with my name on it, welcoming me to Italy. We both laughed as we gave each other our usual bear-hug greeting, and made our way to the car park. It was good to see him. Roberto was the brother I'd never had, and no matter how many months passed between seeing each other, it always felt like we had never parted.

As we drove through the familiar countryside, we reminisced over old times, and laughed about some of the pranks we used to get up to, which all seemed a lifetime ago. As young children, we'd had our share of infantile behaviour, which occasionally caused our parents to resort to disciplining us. We had run through fields and farmyards, causing feathers to fly as we ran amok amongst a range of poultry; even the larger animals would run for shelter. They were good times, which bonded me and Roberto forever.

As we drove through the village, it was alive and buzzing with the daily comings and goings – sure, not "buzzing" in the same context as when one describes Brighton, but buzzing nonetheless, with life and happiness. When the village was enthused it was a shared experience; when Brighton buzzed, everyone was busy among themselves, with no sign of unity and no sense of togetherness.

Here, the streets were occupied by old ladies, their hair

covered by cotton scarves, dressed in dark, crinkling pinafores covering bulging waistlines. They mingled with the Dolce Vita belles, wearing the latest style for the current season, their laughter echoing as they caught up with the latest gossip. These too were joined by high-pitched sounds from the village children, continuous yapping from an under-nourished hound and, not to be left out, the local men taking their evening stroll, to digest the home-cooked meal they had just consumed and enjoy a smoke, whilst eyeing the passing bella females. Soon, I would be part of this – and it felt great!

The following day, after enjoying a hearty lunch, I took a trip down to the local solicitors – better known as the notaries – to complete any last-minute legalities on the purchase of Agostino's house, pay a deposit and wait for the paperwork to be processed. The local notary reassured me that it would not take too long; approximately two weeks for contracts to be exchanged, signed and finalized. But this was Italy; two weeks could mean two months. Patience was the key word, and I had to resign to the fact that renovation on old Agostino's house – my new house – would have to wait a little longer.

I spent this time contacting various local building companies, ordering materials and organizing a team of locals to assist me in my forthcoming project. As in all small towns and villages, it isn't what you know but who you know, and my family were no exception; I was introduced to six local tradesmen who, between them, had the necessary skills to sympathetically renovate my new home.

But, surely, everything went to plan; the *t*s were crossed, the *i*s dotted and contracts were finally exchanged; I was now the proud owner of the house which had been a part of my life from as far back as I could remember.

It had been hot and humid all day, and although the dust hung heavy in the air, and every part of my body ached, there was a satisfying feeling of sheer contentment when I collapsed onto the camp bed, which was purchased for me by Uncle Italo, as a temporary sleeping arrangement.

Eager to finalize all renovations, my life became a blend of early mornings and late nights. By day, no other thought occupied my mind than restoring my new abode, and by night the usual quantity of food and drink was consumed with Roberto and the rest of the family.

Most of the rooms had soon been completed, but old Agostino's bedroom was left until the very last – this room was special to me, and I wanted to give it my undivided attention; it was the room I was most looking forward to bringing back to its natural glory.

The local tradesmen were fantastic, and new friendships had definitely been formed. We parted company with a few drinks and promises to stay in touch.

The following day I began work, stripping away the old plaster and hoping that I would do the room justice, with the skills taught to me over the years.

Once again, as I worked I was drawn to the small, wooden door which was set in the wall.

Legend had it that this miniature "secret door", as it was often referred to by Agostino, was once a tabernacle, used to store Holy Communion wine, bread and water for the monks to carry out daily blessings. The door would open to reveal a ledge with a figurine of the Mother Mary holding Jesus. Thoughts of my conversation with Roberto came flooding back.

Were my eyes deceiving me, or had the wooden door been forced open?

Nono, what happened here?

I would have to resign myself to the idea that the old boy had taken this piece of information with him to his grave.

After another exhausting day, I decided to skip my usual visit to Roberto's, and called him to make my apologies. I made myself comfortable on the camp bed, with a panini purchased earlier in the day for this evening's feast, and a bottle of aqua to wash it down. My eyes looked around the room at what I had accomplished. Time to switch off and get some much-needed shuteye.

Time moved fast, and with most of the work soon completed, my attention turned to the furnishings, which needed to be chosen with the décor of the building in mind. I enjoyed visiting the surrounding villages, foraging through antique shops, searching for the most appropriate trappings to enhance and embellish my home.

Weighed down by a variety of furniture and oddments, I made several trips up the flight of stairs, and deposited them in a disorganized heap on the floor. The larger furniture, such as the two sofas and beds, were going to be delivered the next day.

Before tackling the heap of objects surrounding me, I took a break with a double espresso and biscotti. With my batteries recharged, I began to organize and place my purchases into categories determined by which room they belonged in.

Evening came very quickly, and after a much-needed shower and a bite to eat, I settled on the camp bed and tried to immerse myself in a frivolous novel. Within minutes, my eyelids grew heavy, and I effortlessly fell into a deep sleep.

"Good morning, Roberto. Where's the best place for me to buy wood stain and wood polish? No, not for my hair; very funny! Today, the floorboards in my bedroom are going to get an overhaul."

Roberto gave me the name and directions to a hardware shop in St. Giovanni, a ten-minute drive away. After a quick catch-up, I hung up and got ready for the trip to St. Giovanni.

Before leaving the house, I hit the speed-dial.

"Hello?"

"Danny, it's good to hear your voice. How're things?"

Danny responded loudly: "Great! I've enjoyed the updates you've been sending me. Everyone still asks after you." Danny went on to update me about the business and reassure me that he had everything under control. Before we knew it, without putting any effort into the conversation, an hour had passed. It was good to hear my friend's voice.

There was another hot day ahead, and the sun had already settled high over the terracotta roofs. Village life was in full swing, with the rattle of opening shutters greeting the start of trade at the local establishments. Life here in Terranuova was so different to Brighton, with its screeching traffic at unearthly hours and revellers returning home, interrupting the crack of dawn silence with their yelling and senseless kicking of abandoned missiles. Here, these were replaced by the odd footsteps of someone walking by and an air of the tranquillity I had so longed for.

St. Giovanni was already busy with shoppers. With basket in tow, I perused the aisles looking for all the necessary materials to restore the bedroom floor. A hundred euros lighter, I was soon back at home.

With a change of clothing, I started sanding down the wooden floor with my belt sander. After sweeping away the dust which had been created, the next task was to check and repair the floorboards.

It was at this point that I noticed a section of the floorboards had a groove around them. Closer inspection revealed two screws in the same place. Reaching for a screwdriver, I unscrewed them, revealing a trap door.

My immediate thought was that this was where the electric junction boxes were. Still, I lifted the trap door.

I was surprised to find no junction boxes, but a large tin box. Using my sleeve to dislodge the top coat of dust, I prised open the lid and tentatively peered inside. Whatever I had discovered must have been valuable to Nono, for him to conceal them underneath his floorboards. I pictured the old man and thought fondly of him, as I handled his treasured possessions. The box contained some personal items: documents, a rosary, a non-functioning watch, a few gold rings, a gold cross on a chain, and another chain with two keys, one small and one large, of wrought iron.

There was also an envelope, with my name written in capital letters.

My heart started to race!

I heard footsteps approaching and turned to see Roberto standing in the doorway. My discovery was in full view, so I showed it to him. Together, we inspected the paperwork and the remaining items, including the keys, which had rusted with age. They were heavy in my hand, with small flakes of rust staining my open palm.

I felt an immense sense of sadness. These items were the last remaining possessions of a much-loved man, who had felt it necessary to secure them by hiding them under the floorboards. Roberto said nothing, but I knew that he was having the same thoughts. Agostino was a noble gentleman, whose life had come to an end with only a large tin box as evidence of his existence – and, of course, our never-faltering memories of the old boy. I slipped the envelope addressed to me in my pocket; I wanted to read it alone.

Roberto turned to the reason for his visit: "Nathan, Aunt Marie sent me over to tell you that she won't take no for an answer; she wants you to come over for dinner. She said you can't restore anything living just on paninis."

The letter would have to wait. I quickly washed and changed and left with Roberto.

At dinner, everyone noticed that I was quieter than usual, and decided that it was probably due to overworking. After we ate, Aunt Marie insisted that Roberto take me home, so that I could rest and get an early night.

"Thanks, Auntie. I'll ring you soon."

Finally, I lay on the camp bed and removed the envelope from my pocket.

"My dear Nathan,

If you are reading this letter I have gone to meet my maker. I wanted to make it as easy as possible for you to buy this place one day, without offending Rosa. Rosa was never interested in living in Italy, and I discussed my wishes with her; she obviously kept to my wishes. I have always seen you as my son, and wanted to leave you something special as my final gift.

Remember the stories I often told you, about the treasure hidden behind the secret door? Well, there was some truth in them. The small key opens the wooden door to get into the tabernacle. Inside, remove the figurine of the Virgin Mary holding baby Jesus, and slide the stone base anticlockwise, so that you can remove it. Then insert the larger key in the keyhole below. Nathan, please be careful who you trust, as what you are about to discover is,

I believe, of great value.

Keep safe, my son.

With love, your Nono."

Wow!

Already it was midnight, but sleep was the last thing on my mind.

I did as Nono had instructed, and slipped the large key into the keyhole concealed under the stone base, inside the tabernacle. Then, reaching for my torch, I took a closer look inside the dark opening, where I could see an oblong-shaped item. Carefully, I managed to lift the item out. Suspense filled the air around me. "What have you been hiding, my friend?" I asked, as if Agostino were here with me.

The object was a wooden box, with iron hinges and leather straps. Inside it was a gold cross, encrusted with diamonds, as well as gold rings and chains, which were also embellished with sparkling stones. Inside the lid, a spring lock revealed a dated parchment scroll. I carefully unfolded it, desperately trying not to damage it. It was a drawing of a map, featuring faded crosses and Roman numerals. The legend references were written in Latin, so I believed.

The night heat was beginning to take its toll, so I placed everything back where I had found them and tried to sleep.

For some strange reason I felt lonely, and found myself wishing there was a special someone in my life.

My thoughts drifted to Olivia. She came closest, of any woman I dated, to becoming Mrs. Doyle. Sadly, things came to an abrupt end when she announced that she wanted commitment. Was I not ready, or was I not capable? Whatever it was, there followed the exchange of a few harsh words and tears, before she packed her possessions and was gone. Following previous relationships, I'd been happy to be a singleton, answering to no one, but this time it was different; I missed her. There were numerous times I wanted to call her, but I didn't know what to say. *Nathan Doyle, what an idiot you are!*

On a whim, remembering the time difference, I leant back, scooped up my mobile and scanned through the memory. Then, with slight hesitation, I pressed the call button.

After three rings a familiar, soft voice answered: "Hello, Olivia Somersby."

Plucking up courage, I muttered: "Hi, Olivia. It's Nathan."

There followed a pause, then the phone went dead.

The furniture for the two bedrooms was the last to be delivered, in order to give me time to decorate the rooms. As this was arranged for a few days' time, the floor staining and polishing could wait no longer; I rolled up my shirt sleeves and got to work.

That evening, I unpacked the contents of the tabernacle and placed them on the coffee table. I was not prepared for what stared back at me.

My eyes focused on the gold cross, heavily encrusted with coloured stones. It measured approximately six inches in length and four inches in width, and had substantial weight. I was spellbound by the skilled craftsmanship of this unique cross, with its rare gems. In its centre there was a large emerald, surrounded by a multitude of smaller sapphires and rubies. Why was this mesmerizing beauty hidden, and by whom?

I started to see why Roberto would think Agostino's last tale was true. So far, Roberto only knew about the contents of the tin box found under the floorboards, but not about the items of the tabernacle. My first inclination was to tell Roberto why Agostino had always kept the door locked and the key hidden – after all, we shared everything. However, my initial excitement soon evaporated; Roberto would tell his family and they in turn would tell others – soon, the entire frigging village would know! Agostino's words came back to me: *"Be careful who you trust."* Deciding that I would have to keep this find to myself, I poured myself a glass of wine and reread the letter Agostino wrote to me.

I wondered if he had kept this secret out of respect to the ancient monks. Unfolding the scroll once more, I stared at the indecipherable hieroglyphics, and wished I had been a model student in my Latin classes; this was well beyond my capabilities.

The phone rang, and I immediately mentally reminded myself not to tell Roberto about the second lot of items. I picked up the receiver.

"What on Earth made you call me, after all this time?"

Surprised, I could only utter: "Sorry."

"Sorry? Is that why you called me? To say sorry?"

"No, I mean sorry for calling so late. I called you because… I was thinking about you. About us. I called because I miss you."

"What do you want me to say, Nathan? I wanted more and you didn't."

"Maybe losing you was what it took for me to realize what you meant… what you *mean* to me. I just know I want you in my life."

The line went quiet for a while, and I thought again that she was going to hang up. Then, Olivia replied: “Next time you’re in London, look me up.”

Chapter 2

London streets are always bustling, with everyone looking as if they have a purpose, and none more so than Kensington in rush hour.

It was a pleasant summer's evening. Office workers were escaping their duties for another day, early theatre goers were filling the overpriced bistros, and elegant hotels were welcoming their newly arriving guests. The ornate black and gold gates of Kensington Palace Gardens invited strolling couples in to view the abundance of floral arrangements; the Albert Memorial was being photographed from every angle.

This had been our old stomping ground, and I was determined to find Olivia, who I hoped was still a creature of habit. I scoured the most obvious haunts, which we often frequented, and places where I knew Olivia met up with friends. Luck was on my side; I soon caught a glimpse of her, sitting by the window in Nick the Greek's Taverna. She was shielded slightly by her journalist colleagues, and so engrossed in their jovial conversation, that she did not notice me as I walked past her and headed for the bar.

Before anybody thinks I'd gone soft, I actually came back to England to see Danny, and to put my house up for sale; I just took the opportunity to see Olivia, too. Well, that's my story and I'm sticking to it!

I sat on a bar stool directly opposite her, waiting to see how long it would take her to notice me. Olivia looked, as always, stylish and stunning, in a pair of designer jeans and a pale blue shirt, provocatively unbuttoned. She was sipping a Mojito cocktail with mountains of ice and sprigs of mint, whilst sharing a basket of pita bread and various Greek dips.

The barman seemed happy to see me. "Hello. Long time no see! Where have you been, my friend?"

I replied: "It's a long story, but it's good to be back."

"What can I get you?"

"Can I have a nice cold Mythos, please?"

"Of course, my friend. You know Olivia is here, too?"

"Yes, I know."

I turned my bar stool around and watched her, as I reminisced over times gone by.

Olivia was taking a sip of her drink, when her eyes looked up in my direction. She put her glass down and sat for a while staring at me, without any expression on her face. I smiled and, without saying a word, gestured for her to join me. As she continued to stare at me, I wondered what she would do. I hoped she was able to pick up the messages my brain was sending to hers, pleading with her to come over and talk for a while. My mind and body started feeling the adrenaline between us, and I quietly thanked the powers of telepathy, as I watched her walk toward me. Her dazzling blue eyes focused on mine momentarily, and I pulled a bar stool near to me, for her to sit.

Without asking, the barman placed a second glass of Mythos and a Mojito on the bar, in front of us. "On the house. It's good to see you both again." We both smiled and thanked him for the drinks.

"What are you doing here, Nathan?" she asked.

Mischievously, I responded: "Well, I was in the area, so I thought I would call in for a beer. I had no idea you would still be using this joint."

"Really?" Olivia replied.

"In our last phone call you said to look you up when I was in London, so here I am."

We spent the next half an hour making polite conversation, before I impatiently interrupted her: "I'm glad to hear that you're not dating. I've missed you so much."

As we sat in silence, the multitude of emotions scampering through my mind were extremes, ranging from elation to regret. To me, Olivia was the epitome of womanhood, beautiful inside and out, stylish and confident, knowledgeable and inquisitive, with a mischievous nature and humour which melted my heart. Okay, admittedly, as I remembered she was also stubborn, hard work and a terrible cook! Realization of just how much I had missed her hit me like a thunderbolt.

Some of Olivia's colleagues came over to say goodnight, and ask if she wanted a lift home. Olivia looked at me; without saying a word I was subconsciously pleading with her to say that she was okay and stay. She walked back to where her friends were sitting, collected her cardigan and bag, then walked back to me.

"Have you eaten?" I asked.

"No, just a few dips."

"Will you stay for dinner with me?"

She hesitated, then nodded; "Okay."

We stayed at Nick the Greek's Taverna until closing time.

After, we bade our old friend goodnight and promised not to leave it so long until the next time. Then we made our way home.

Time had passed, but the spark which had kept us together for nearly three years was most definitely still there in abundance. Without uttering a syllable, we joined hands and walked in unison to her mews apartment, tucked away in a secluded, leafy street. Olivia opened the black gloss-painted door, heavily embellished with brass work, which framed the cool, marbled hallway, in wait inside for everyone to admire.

"It was good to see you, Nathan. Thanks for dinner and thanks for coming."

That was my cue to leave. I kissed her on the cheek and walked away.

This was the first night in a long time that my mind was not on the mission I had committed myself to.

As soon as I was back at my room, I reached for the phone and sent Olivia a text, thanking her for a great evening, and asking with trepidation if she would like to meet up for dinner tomorrow night.

My phone lit up quickly, and eagerly I read Olivia's reply: *"7 o'clock at our taverna?"*

I agreed, smirking to myself: *our* taverna!

Nick smiled at us mischievously, adding, as he was showing us to our seats: “Welcome. It’s good to see you back together.” Neither of us replied.

We spent the evening catching up and reminiscing.

Olivia was intrigued with Agostino’s treasures. Then, she suspiciously asked: “Hang on a minute! Have you come to see me just because you need a translator?”

“Olivia, I know you studied Latin, but come on… it wouldn’t be difficult to find someone else to translate the manuscripts for me... in Italy! I just wanted to see you. I suppose I’m hoping you will consider giving us a second chance.”

Olivia took a deep sigh and replied: “Perhaps.”

I ordered a bottle of Champagne and we drank a toast to the future.

We reached Olivia’s abode and I followed her into the marbled hall, waiting for the lift to come down. An elderly woman, very slight in physique, joined us in the lift, and seemed to wedge herself and her oversized tartan shopping bag between us, which amused both Olivia and I.

Olivia’s elegant apartment was faultless and everything had its place. There was an ornate wooden shelf by the front door, to place shoes on, as the apartment was furnished with soft, cream, shag-pile carpet throughout.

Without uttering a word, Olivia walked toward me, placed a kiss on my lips and headed straight to the bedroom. I needed no persuading to follow, unbuttoning clothes and discarding them wherever they fell.

We allowed our naked bodies to entwine, making love slowly and meaningfully. It felt right, it felt great and it was magical.

"When are you going back to Italy?"

"By the end of the week."

We could hear the clock ticking, and perhaps our heartbeats, too.

"I'm due a vacation. Maybe I can visit you."

"Do you mean it?"

Olivia smiled and I held her tightly against me. "Well, you do need a translator, and I am definitely intrigued with your findings out there, so why not?"

"You have made me a very happy man. You won't regret it."

Over breakfast, we made plans. Olivia would take time out

from her freelance journalism, I would pass the day-to-day running of the business to Danny, and together we would go back to Italy.

Chapter 3

With so much occupying my mind, I left the matter of hiring a car until we arrived at Pisa airport. The choice was now limited, but beggars can't be choosers, so I paid the deposit and loaded our luggage into the red Fiat Bravo. It was obvious to see why the car fell in the low budget hire-car category, mainly due to its age, and it did not include any extras.

Once back in Terranuova, I took Olivia to meet the family. She had been to Italy before, but had never met the family en masse, and in particular had not yet been introduced to Uncle Italo and Aunt Marie. Olivia knew that meeting my aunt and uncle signified my commitment to her. We joined the family in the dining room, where there was a feast spread across the large wooden dining table – a banquet fit for a king and his queen.

Roberto was in good spirits, and kept Olivia amused with his stories from the past; his raucous laugh bellowed throughout the room. The food kept on coming, the wine flowed and I felt at ease with the world.

Olivia looked stunning, her huge mass of curls piled high on her head, very little make-up and a simple halter-neck sundress accentuating her sensational figure. The women of the family whisked Olivia away, no doubt to extract any worthwhile piece of gossip. This is an area in which I envy the female species; any language barrier did not seem to hinder communication.

The evening passed amiably. Roberto played his harmonica badly, while the rest of us sat around chatting, and wishing we had refrained from over-indulging ourselves. As I looked around the room, over the faces of all the people I loved, I felt a strange apprehension, and silently wished that this feeling of contentment would last forever.

Once back at home, I took Olivia by the hand and led her to where the tabernacle was. I opened the tabernacle with the iron key and carefully lifted the precious contents from inside, laying the scroll and pouch containing the gold cross atop the uneven wooden kitchen table. Slowly, I unfolded the scroll, using two old spanners and a hammer which were littering the floor, to keep the corners from rolling together. The evening was hot and humid, with the dying sun streaming shafts of intermittent light across the old document. Olivia scanned every symbol, sign and mark in silence, deep in concentration at the works, which were possibly written several centuries ago, and may contain secrets of their time.

I removed the gold cross from the worn leather pouch and laid it gently beside the scroll. It had to be worth a substantial amount; the abundant precious stones were absolutely breathtaking. Olivia gently lifted the cross into the last ray of light; the jewels shimmered and sparkled as she gently rotated the cross, turning it over and over to inspect every angle.

The realization that we were embarking on something exceptional seized our very souls.

The next morning, we were woken by the usual commuting of the locals going about their business, and forced ourselves to get up and begin the eventful day we had planned. We both still felt the effects of the night before, the lack of sleep and, of course, the questions concerning where our scrolls would lead us. It was important to ascertain the meaning of the ancient words and symbols, and the value of the cross, but more importantly how they had come to be hidden in the old tabernacle. And, did Agostino have any connections to the schemes of the past?

Roberto called to say that he had spruced up a Mini Cooper, and it was ready for me to pick it up sometime before midday, as he was closing early. After a hasty breakfast consisting of steaming coffee and stale paninis, we made plans to pick up the Mini. Olivia would then follow me back to Pisa to drop off the hire car, and we would make our way to Firenze.

Little was said during our drive through olive groves and the beautiful countryside. The only other form of life was a solitary old man with a brace of dishevelled donkeys, toiling slowly along a parched, unmarked track.

Once in Firenze, I dropped Olivia at the library, so that she could begin researching through archives. Translating the document would take time, and she was best left alone to concentrate fully on the task at hand. I helped her carry as many old reference books as were available to an empty table, then made myself scarce.

I spent most of the day traversing the antique shops of this famous old city, and found some interesting items to enhance my new abode. As time was on my side, I took advantage by gazing with avid interest at jewellery on the Gold Bridge, hoping to get some kind of inkling as to the value of the cross, but without any success; its uniqueness and quality by far superseded anything on display.

My eyes locked onto a platinum ring, with a set of three

circles encrusted with black diamonds. Its slanting shape made it clear that it was not to be worn on the left hand, so there would be no mistaking it as an engagement ring. I wanted to buy Olivia something special to represent my commitment to her, but I didn't want to move too fast, either.

The sales assistant came toward me and said: "Ah, the promise ring. Lovely, isn't it?"

"Can you wrap it for me?"

"Of course. She's a lucky lady."

I smiled and hoped Olivia would like it, too.

By the time I went to collect Olivia, her hair was tousled, with strands of hair escaping from the clip which had held it all in place. Discarded plastic cups, presumably once filled with water, surrounded masses of paperwork; my girl was totally engrossed in the job at hand. She was tired but jubilant, in as much as she had decoded some of the keywords, and was beginning to put sentences together.

It was late in the day when we were informed that the library was closing, and that all files had to be returned to their rightful places. Gathering all the important paperwork together, we left in silence, hand in hand.

Only when safely seated in a local pizzeria, munching our way through the menu, did we speak. We huddled together in secrecy, whispering to each other, wanting no one to hear our conversation.

Olivia began by saying: "Nathan, as we predicted, the scroll is hundreds of years old. It was written to a priest, by the cardinal. It appears that funds were being raised for a war, and great deals of resources were needed; the bishop is encouraging Italian nobles to contribute to 'the cause', confidentiality being of the utmost importance. The map on the scroll seems to bear references to churches and places of worship throughout Italy; I need time to investigate deeper the significance of the places marked on the scroll.

"It seems there was a plot – a conspiracy, perhaps even treason – being planned, and I need to understand exactly what the scroll is referring to."

I sat calmly listening to what Olivia told me, trying hard to comprehend what I was hearing. Suddenly, food seemed to be of little consequence. My brain went into overdrive, and I found myself unable to fathom what such important documents, so dangerous in the wrong hands, were doing in Agostino's belongings. I wanted suddenly to get back to the seclusion of home.

Driving home, Olivia slid down into the leather seat and slipped into a comfortable snooze, little puffs of breath escaping periodically from the corner of her open mouth. As the car bumped along through the dark countryside, the air conditioning failed to operate, so I wound the window down low, allowing myself to feel the wind blowing through my hair, and helping me to focus on the road ahead. I started to realize that, the more we uncovered, the deeper into the unknown we were heading. The innocence of the secret tabernacle had now turned sinister, tinged with intrigue and collusion.

By the time we arrived back in Terranuova, it was dark, with many shutters firmly shut tight for the night, and the inhabitants safely tucked up in their beds. Once home, we emptied our bags and lay on the couch, side by side, deep in thoughts of what the true meaning of the scroll might signify. There was clearly more than a small possibility that our lives would be transformed from now onward.

It was then that I remembered the promise ring, which I purchased in Firenze. As we got into bed, I took Olivia's right hand and slipped the ring onto her finger.

“What’s this for?” she asked.

“It’s a promise ring, until we hopefully take our relationship to the next step.”

Olivia kissed me, and we fell asleep in each other’s arms.

Chapter 4

Another restless night, and my thoughts turned to an old buddy of mine, Eddie Morrissey. Eddie was in the antique jewellery trade, and had rented and owned antique jewellery shops in many areas of England.

It had been a good few years since I last saw Eddie, and hoped he hadn't changed his mobile number. I dialled the number, and waited when it went to the answering service.

"Hi, Eddie. Sorry, mate, you must still be asleep. It's Nathan. Give me a call when you get this message." What was I thinking? It was three o'clock in the morning here; two o'clock back in England!

The last time I saw Eddie, he was trading in a backstreet establishment in Bethnal Green. But I trusted Eddie implicitly, and felt that maybe he could help me date and value the gold cross. It obviously had a significant monetary worth; it was not your run of the mill trinket, to bandy around.

Eddie was always ducking and diving; even ex-wives hounded him for alimony, all of whom he managed to keep at bay and avoid payment of any sort. Tall and suave, he had mischievous, twinkling blue eyes, with a mop of blond hair slicked back off his face. Eddie had an obsession for silk shirts of every colour, good quality suits and handmade shoes, which put the rest of us men to shame. His nickname was "Nifty", partly due to his impeccable dress sense and partly due to his personality. I met Eddie through our shared love of antiques; his bag was gold, silver and jewellery and mine was clocks, period furniture and select ornate pieces of interest. Eddie had many contacts, and could pull off a deal to match the best in the business. It was a friendship that could not be measured by time spent together, but by the sheer understanding that, however much time lapsed, either one of us could pick up the phone and it would be as if we had only seen each other the day before.

I was watching Olivia as she slept when the phone rang. It was Eddie's number.

"Nifty, how're you doing, you old rogue?"

"Oh, this and that; nothing much has changed. You?" Eddie asked.

"Long story, but I'm good."

We caught up a little and I discovered that, for once, Eddie was living alone. "I'm looking for the right girl. I suppose you could say I've matured somewhat." We both chuckled in disbelief.

I went on to explain why I'd called in the early hours of the morning.

"I'm living in Italy now, and was wondering if you fancied a short vacation; I need your expertise on a piece I've come across. Of course, I'll make it worth your time."

I knew Eddie would be intrigued, and he agreed to call me in a day or two with dates.

Olivia blinked and stretched her bare arms over her head, pushing back her ruffled hair, which had fallen over her beautiful face. My instinct was to join her under the covers, but time was pressing, as Olivia was going back to London in a few weeks, and we still had so much to do.

We left the village early and drove to Firenze again.

I dropped Olivia back at the library, to continue unravelling the secrets of the scroll. It was a long and tedious job, best left to Olivia, whose knowledge of Latin was far superior to mine. The look on Olivia's face showed how much she enjoyed delving through the dust-laden shelves of books revealing the history of the past; she was in her element cross-referencing and abstracting information from one ancient book to another.

I checked in with Danny, to see how things were going with the business. It seemed that all was well, with the exception of his missing me.

"Thanks, mate. I miss you, too. But it seems you're coping admirably without me on site." We talked for a while and agreed to Skype soon.

Maybe it was time to consider letting go of the business and enjoy a new lifestyle – after all, I classed Terranuova as home now; I knew I could be happy here.

I also knew that the gold cross had to be worth a fortune, but where could an item so conspicuous be sold, and to whom?

My mind was jumping from one thing to another.

Olivia was sitting on the steps leading to the library, when I pulled up.

"Hi. You okay?" I asked.

"More than okay, darling. I will reveal all later. Right now I'm famished; what's for dinner?"

We drove home making only small-talk, as it was impossible

to have a meaningful discussion driving through the rush-hour traffic of Firenze.

When we returned, Terranuova was alive with sounds of merriment. A local wedding had taken place earlier in the day, and the continuation of celebration was evident throughout the piazza.

Cousin Roberto and other family members were making their way back home, when Roberto spotted us and walked toward us, greeting us with one of his infamous bear hugs. I kissed my cousin's wife Paolla, Auntie Marie and Uncle Italo, and promised that we would come over the next day for coffee, as today we were pretty tired from driving back and forth to Firenze. Then, as quickly as I could, I made our excuses and whisked Olivia away to the solitude of home.

Once inside, we battened down the shutters, opened a bottle of chilled Chianti and ordered a margherita pizza and garlic bread, to be delivered; Olivia made up a bowl of salad to accompany our takeaway.

After, we cleared the newly-arrived oak dinner table of the leftover remnants of our meal, so that Olivia could spread the scroll and reams of paperwork in an orderly manner. Huddled together, we shuffled the papers about, trying to make sense of what was written. Olivia began to tell me what she had managed to unravel so far.

"I believe there was a war being planned against the English monarchy, and that money and valuables were being gathered to raise funds to finance this."

Olivia continued to explain that this would have been in the 16th century, as Cardinal Bertocelli is mentioned on the scroll, and he mysteriously disappeared around the year 1537. In fact, several cardinals throughout Italy disappeared at the same time.

Olivia went on to say: "It is written that all funds were to be safeguarded at places of worship, until they could be collected by Cardinal Bertocelli's emissaries."

It had become apparent from what Olivia was saying that, according to the scroll, people were incensed that King Henry VIII, to fulfil his own selfish needs, took it upon himself to dissolve the Catholic Church and create a new Church of England; this would also automatically make him the head of the Church. Although greatly displeased, the pope had no desire to go to war with England; therefore it fell to the bishops and cardinals of Italy to gather in secret, and form a coalition to overthrow the English throne.

It seemed quite possible that a great deal of this treasure was hidden or buried throughout Italy; now it made sense that the gold cross was hidden in a tabernacle, in a property which used to be a monastery.

This information was hard to comprehend; it was late and the day had taken its toll on both of us. We both knew there would be repercussions from uncovering the implications of the scroll, much greater than just treasure; perhaps even a conspiracy of treason.

"Nathan, do you know what this means?"

"Yes, there's a vast amount of treasure and other valuables hidden throughout the Italian countryside, just waiting to be discovered. More importantly, the history attached to such a mission opens so many questions, like how long has it all lay hidden, and how many lives have been lost because of it. Is it possible that there was a planned uprising against the king of England, Henry VIII, from the hierarchy of Italian nobles, and was this with or without the pope's blessing? Either way, this was a scandalous crime against the British throne. Olivia, surely such actions would be deemed a conspiracy?"

It was impossible to comprehend that something so immense was within our grasp; that we were so close to uncovering a dark secret buried hundreds of years ago, which could have changed the course of history forever. I was determined to find out more, and unravel the enigma surrounding the scroll: why the funds were being gathered, and what became of the group of cardinals who vanished into thin air. My mind was in turmoil, unable to accept that Italy was so opposed to the king of England that they plotted to have him overthrown from his throne, because of his beliefs and actions.

The next day, Eddie called.

"Mate, is your offer of a vacation still open?"

"Yes, you can come over?"

"Yes, mate, I can come over, but only for a few days."

I made all the arrangements for Eddie, and met him at Pisa airport, a couple of days later.

"Great to see you! You haven't changed at all."

"Nor have you, mate. Bought you your favourite fruit nougat from Dave's sweetshop."

"Thanks, mate, I'll have some after we've eaten."

We chatted all the way back to Terranuova.

Olivia prepared dinner and we sat around the table, laughing and discussing both past and present.

It turned into another long day for all of us, so we decided to head for bed and discuss the gold cross in the morning.

Eddie was already dressed when I came into the sitting room the next day. He seemed eager to see the famous gold cross.

He took out his loupe to study the workmanship, and the type of gold it was made from.

"Nathan, this is definitely a rare piece; judging by the gold used and the lack of hallmarks it must be centuries old. How did the old man come to own it?"

"No idea, mate, but I think there's every possibility that I will unravel more with every new piece of information I obtain."

"Nathan, it's worth a fortune! And I know a man who would be interested in a piece like this. Many people wouldn't touch an item of this calibre, but I have a friend in Antwerp who will give you a fair price. I'll contact him and see if we can arrange a meeting with him."

"Thanks, mate."

Olivia was heading back to London in a few days, and it occurred to me that this was probably for the best; it would give me time to meet up with Eddie's friend, and not have to worry for

Olivia's safety.

Eddie called his contact later that day.

"Hi, can you put me through to Fredrik Fritz, please? Just say it's Nifty."

After some discussion, Eddie hung up and relayed the conversation to me. Eddie's friend Fredrik Fritz lived in Antwerp, which was perhaps a healthy distance from Italy, as discretion was paramount. The less people in the know, the better; there was too much at risk, and I didn't want to involve anyone unnecessarily. But, if Eddie thought we needed him, then I knew we did. We agreed to meet the following weekend at the Eden Savoy Hotel, which stands close to the business district in Antwerp. This gave me four whole days to study the map and the markings on the scroll – after all, it was without doubt what would lead us to discover the rest of the treasure.

"I've managed to get a flight tomorrow, at eleven-thirty in the morning;" Olivia announced, going on to say, "this will give you boys time to concentrate on your plans."

I looked over at her and smiled. "How long will you be gone?"

"About two weeks. Hopefully, by then you will be back from Antwerp and ready for the next stage."

Chapter 5

I took Olivia to the airport, and felt a pang of regret as she walked reluctantly toward the departure gate. "Call me as soon as you land," I told her with a kiss, and watched her hand her passport over. She turned back and I blew her another kiss, watching as she pretended to catch it.

Eddie was out by the time I got back, probably chatting up the locals.

I sat alone in my sitting room, with the scroll spread in front of me, trying to make sense of the markings, which were so faded they were hard to see. I opened the tabernacle and sat holding the gold cross in the palm of my hand, turning it over and over. I imagined a time when this could have been hidden away in a secure hiding place, awaiting collection by a paid courier, so that it could be used against the king of England, to contribute to his downfall. But why had it never been collected? Who had placed it in the tabernacle and what had become of that person?

Fortunately, I had a map of the local area, and I studied it intensely. I needed to bear in mind that, in years gone by, many of today's places would not have existed, so markings on the old scroll would need to be placed in the locality on the current map. There were unclear markings on the scroll, which made me think of the general lie of the land close to Terranuova. Maybe if I made a note of possible churches, monasteries and other places of worship, they might fit into the pattern of the map, hopefully interpret correctly and uncover the undisclosed hiding places where the valuable commodities were buried, which would have changed history.

It was early evening by the time I had finally decided to call it a day.

The phone rang. It was Olivia, letting me know that she had arrived safely and missed me already.

I heard the door close and Eddie came up the stairs, holding a bag of groceries and a bottle of vino.

"Hello, mate, what's all this?"

Eddie responded: "I thought you might be a little jaded after your trip to the airport, so I'm cooking us dinner."

"You can cook?"

"Of course I can cook! I've been living on my own for the past five years."

It was great catching up with Eddie, but as usual our minds

went back to the gold cross, getting it valued and optimistically hoping to sell it, to fund the continuation of this quest.

"Oh, I forgot to tell you, Fredrik called me and he is definitely interested. I told him I was only around for a few days, so he can see us as soon as we like."

With Olivia back in London, it made sense to move as fast as we could. We discussed the various methods of transport and their implications, and decided that the best method was to drive to Antwerp.

"It's only eight o'clock; if we get an early night we could be in Antwerp by the afternoon," said Eddie.

"Sounds good to me."

With that, we set our alarm clocks and called it a night.

The drive to Belgium was uneventful.

As Eddie knew the area better than me, I left the arrangements to him. He booked us into the Astrid Hotel in Antwerp, which is centrally located in the heart of the world-famous diamond area, and stands opposite the monumental Antwerp Central station and zoo. The hotel was modern, airy and contemporary in decor.

Not wanting to draw any attention to ourselves, we booked in and went straight to our room. We ordered a bite to eat and, after refreshing ourselves, headed straight to Fredrik's shop. Nifty Eddie lived up to his reputation by choosing a snappy, grey designer suit, with an open-neck, pale pink shirt and hand-crafted Italian shoes for our meeting.

"Steady on, mate; he'll think we're loaded!" I chose less formal attire.

And, we were on our way.

Eddie had arranged for us to meet at two-thirty, with the infamous Fredrik Fritz. We arrived at a non-descript jewellery store, down a side road about twenty minutes away from Antwerp station. I felt slightly uneasy about the situation, and wished I had something in the way of protection with me. I breathed out a sigh of relief when my brain reminded me that this was a trusted friend of Eddie's.

Fredrik greeted us in perfect English. He was a small, scrawny individual, with a nervous tic which gave the impression that he was continually nodding. We were invited to enter an adjoining room, which had a slight musty smell, and was stuffed from floor to ceiling with packing boxes.

Sitting in a corner of the room was an over-bloated character who answered to the name of Hendrik. His clothing was at least a whole size too small for him, with his overweight stomach hanging over his trouser waistline and his bare midriff poking through every buttonhole on his shirt. Breathing heavily and sweating profusely, Hendrik rasped a greeting which was fairly indistinguishable. Fredrik did all of the talking, and made overtures to Hendrik, as though he was some kind of godfather figure.

Then, with a snap of his fingers, Hendrik indicated that he wanted to view the merchandise. I felt irritated by the whole mafioso vibe surrounding me, but decided that, under the circumstances, it was probably best not to show my annoyance; it might not be healthy. Instead, I dug deep into my battered attaché case and produced the original crumbling leather pouch, passing it over to Hendrik reverently; I noticed that he made no eye contact with me, as the cross and diamond rings slithered from its casing into his hand.

Momentarily, there was a trace of astonishment on his face, but any expression soon vanished back to its original poker state. Hendrik studied the cross with the aid of his eyeglass, twisting it many times to see every facet. He then unceremoniously handed it to Fredrik, who was twitching nervously, even without the added trait of his tic.

Eddie and I glanced at each other in silence. He began to pace the room, which was lit with just a single low-wattage lightbulb; the lighting gave the packing boxes the appearance of giant rocks, which could crash down and pin us to the bare floorboards at any moment. Our imagination may have started to run riot.

After what seemed like a lifetime, Fredrik took the floor. "Eddie, Mr. Doyle, I suppose you are wondering why my friend Hendrik has joined us? After my conversation with Eddie, I realized that the merchandise may be out of my price range, so I invited Hendrik to join us; it may be worth more than I am prepared to offer. But, there are not many people who would consider such an item, so I would urge you to accept thirty-thousand euros."

Before I could react, Eddie snapped: "It's worth at least sixty!"

There was a moment's silence, and again the feeling of uncertainty. The two men started whispering in French. Then, Hendrik removed a further twenty-thousand euros from his pocket. "Our absolute final offer. Take it or leave it; no more will be offered."

I replied: "That's a very good offer, gentlemen, but—"

Eddie interrupted me: "What about the rings? We can let you

have them as a job lot, for a further twenty-five-thousand euros; sixty for the cross and you can have a steal at twenty-five for the rings. Have we got a deal?"

After some theatrical consideration, with a nod and a handshake, the deal was sealed.

Before we reached for the door, Fredrik asked how the cross had come into my possession. I had no intention of giving him any information as to its history – all I wanted was to be as far away from this stuffy storeroom as possible, and even farther from these two characters – so I muttered something absurd about it being in my grandmother's jewellery box, turning the doorknob at the same time. I immediately headed for the safety of the street.

Once we got to the more familiar and populated area near the river, we slowed our pace, and only then did we check behind us to make sure that we were not followed. I started to breathe normally again and looked over at Eddie, who seemed as nervous as me – after all, it's not every day one has 85,000 euros in their pocket.

We leant against the railings of the River Meuse and watched it speedily rolling along. We didn't speak for a while.

Then, Eddie casually asked: "Since when did you have a rich

grandmother?" We laughed and headed back to the hotel.

For a single item to be worth 60,000 euros, I was starting to think something seriously heavy might be about to go down; when the price is this high, danger surely follows!

We headed back to Pisa at the crack of dawn. Eddie was heading straight back to Bethnal Green.

Over the last few days, I'd got the impression that not a lot was happening in Eddie's world, so I took the chance to put a proposition to him: "Eddie, how would you like to be part of uncovering the conspiracy with me – and, of course, earning a stake in the wealth I hope to discover?"

After a short pause, Eddie nodded his head and added: "It's been a long time since I have felt this excited about anything, Nathan; count me in."

Chapter 6

Once back home in Terranuova, I felt more comfortable.

The thick, brown envelope that I had plucked from Hendrik's podgy hands felt surreal. I had counted the contents twice; indeed there were 85,000 euros in clean, crisp notes. I put it inside the tabernacle for safekeeping, knowing that this would be the money to fund the next few months. I took out the pad I bought when visiting Firenze, and made an entry of the 85,000 euros and what it represented; I had decided that every element of this journey would be documented.

Outside in the piazza, the village was heaving with people conducting their everyday activities. The congenial banter – shutters being raised, merchants opening their premises after a short break for lunch – was all so normal, but I had a hunch that things would not really be quite so innocent in the forthcoming days.

My days were spent driving around areas mentioned on the map, hoping that buildings erected since the ancient map and scroll were made would not hinder us finding the buried treasure. My first stop was in the tiny hamlet of Loro Ciuffenna.

It was an excessively warm day, and the need to be in the shade was overwhelming. After parking the car in the shade courteously offered by an accommodating walnut tree, I walked along the cobbled streets, in search of something refreshing to drink. It was early afternoon and the village was quiet, with almost all forms of life taking the sensible option and avoiding the afternoon sun. Balconies had a variety of colour draped over them: bedclothes airing and freshly laundered clothes blowing in the summer breeze, amidst endless terracotta flowerpots, with the esteemed favourite of geraniums cascading in abundance. The streets were too narrow to accommodate vehicles, other than the Vespa scooters parked symmetrically in the designated area.

I quenched my thirst in the one café-bar which was still open, and munched on a semi-stale focaccia and salami panini. The place was shaded, cool and particularly quiet, which encouraged the owner to enter into a deep and meaningful conversation with me. I took the opportunity to engage him regarding ancient churches and other places of worship. He said that the most ancient and visited church in this neighbourhood was in nearby

Borro, and was well worth visiting. He went on to inform me that it was steeped in history, and to make sure I took photos to show my folks, as it was very attractive and impressive.

On his advice, I took a slow drive east through narrow country lanes, where farmers were eking out a meagre living growing crops in dust-blown fields. The medieval town of Borro was not too far, and I was there in no time.

I headed straight toward the church, which was located at the far end of the town. The sun was still shining and the town was alive with a blend of locals and a crowd of tourists, wearing the familiar bum-bags strapped to their waists, and cameras dangling from their necks. The church was imposing in stature, with a huge, open steeple which housed an enormous bell. I entered the church in silence and walked toward the altar, observing in reverence the beauty and splendour of the building.

Cameras flashed intermittently, capturing every aspect of the interior, from its windows to its altar, to the decorative ceiling. Feeling like one of the many tourists, I followed suit and brought out a small Samsung digital camera with tape recording facilities, snapping away happily. However, unlike the other tourists, I also recorded myself narrating the outlay of the church and description regarding its intricate architecture, in detail, as if I were a journalist.

I wished Olivia were here with me, and sent her a text to this effect. She replied she would be back soon – and, it seemed, Nifty too.

I had made arrangements to call Olivia every night at 10.00 p.m. Italian time, but that night Olivia called me.

"Hi, I couldn't wait to tell you that I'm free to fly back earlier than expected."

I was just as excited about this as she was. "When do you need picking up, my lady?"

"How does tomorrow evening sound?"

"Like music to my ears." It seemed that I was going to be chauffeuring backward and forward from the airport for some time.

The next day, I arrived at Pisa airport with a small bouquet of freesias, Olivia's favourite flower.

We drove straight home and made frothy cappuccinos, sitting back ready to exchange our news.

Thinking I was alone, Roberto called to see if I was coming by for dinner. I informed him that Olivia was back, and said we would both pop over tomorrow for coffee, instead.

It was good to have her in my arms again.

*

I had the pictures I had taken at Borro enlarged, and Olivia typed out the audio recording I made, so that we could also have that transcribed in print.

A few days later I received a call from Eddie, to say that he had sorted out the rental of the shop and the flat, and he was ready to come over. "A friend of mine is going to sublet the shop and flat from me, so my bags are packed and I'm ready to rock and roll."

"Okay, mate, let me have the details and chauffeur Nathan will be there."

I didn't want Olivia to think this was going to be a permanent arrangement, so I would start looking for alternative accommodation for Eddie as soon as he got back.

In fact, when I picked Eddie up, he broached the subject of renting his own place before I had mentioned it to him.

"There's no hurry, Eddie. Best we speak to Roberto first; he'll know plenty of people to approach, and the price won't be inflated."

When we got back, we were greeted with smells of fresh herbs and spices, and echoes of sizzling meat being cooked; classical music added to the ambience.

After dinner, Olivia brought out the pile of photos I took on my trip to Borro earlier in the week. "Let's see if your photography skills are as impressive as mine," she joked.

Eddie showed polite interest as she passed him each glossy print, while I attended to the important job of refilling our glasses. I gazed with fascination at the shots over Olivia's shoulder.

Suddenly, one of the photos made me stop and look more intently – a shot taken inside the church, of the altar. As Olivia was passing the photo to Eddie I grabbed it from her hand, adding: "Just want to take a closer look at something."

I brought the photo nearer to the light to examine it closer, then asked Olivia to pass me any other photos taken of the same area. My eyes were transfixed on the altar, and the stone statues which were so prominent: one of the Virgin Mary, draped in a veil, and the other of Jesus Christ, with his hands outstretched. Behind the statues were tabernacles, similar to my very own; they stood proudly on adjacent stone walls, framing the step leading up to the altar. The more I stared, the more I convinced myself that they were the same; if treasure was hidden in my tabernacle, then just maybe treasure was concealed here, too. I showed the photos to Olivia and Eddie, proclaiming that they were the same shape and size, and what I was thinking.

"Well, I doubt if anything is still there now, Nathan," Eddie proclaimed. He could see I was serious and added: "But, we don't lose anything to take a look."

Something in my brain was niggling at me, but the conversation quickly changed to days of yesteryear, and the photos were restored to the flap-wallet and cast aside. There was already a feeling of solidarity, as Eddie and Olivia cleared the table and engaged in idle chatter over the kitchen sink, one washing up and the other drying.

My thoughts drifted to the money stashed away in the tabernacle, and the events of the past few days. How many lives must have been sacrificed to protect the conspiracy they were planning? Sobering thoughts, indeed.

The next morning, Olivia wanted to spend some time on the research she had completed, before her trip to London, and said that she would see us both later.

Prior to our trip to Borro, Eddie and myself made a detour to Roberto's house, to ask if he could make some enquiries regarding flat rentals for Eddie.

"Leave it with me; I will make some telephone calls. I'm sure Eddie will have a place by the end of the week."

We thanked him and went on to Borro. My gut feeling was telling me that today was going to be memorable one.

By the time we had reached the church, it was heaving with tourists and worshippers, which made it difficult, to say the least, to investigate the authenticity of the tabernacle doors. We both concluded that, without a doubt, the tabernacle doors resembled mine, and were possibly built by the same stonemason. I wanted to come back when the church was empty, to examine both tabernacles closer.

Eddie and I scouted around the perimeter and boundaries of the ancient church, jotting down notes about security, the layout and possible areas to gain entry, other than the main doors.

We stopped for a bite to eat and some lubrication at a nearby café, where we mulled over when would be the best time to return, to complete our investigations. We were faced with two possibilities: return at night and break in, or find a reason which would be palatable to the priest, to open up for us when nobody else was there. The latter was our first choice, but unfortunately we couldn't come up with a reason the priest might go for.

The overwhelming feeling that something was waiting to be discovered enveloped me all day, and my anticipation was second to none.

On our return home, Olivia was soaking herself, with a variety of fragrances and bubbles in the bath. She was feeling a little tired and decided to have an early night. This gave us boys the chance to plan our next move regarding gaining entry to the church in Borro.

We both agreed that there was no other solution than to break into the church in the middle of the night.

We made a list of the tools needed for our break-in and ticked them off, one by one, as we placed them into the sack-cloth bag I had found in the basement (or, better known in Italy as the cantina); there, we had also both found dark clothing to help disguise ourselves. We decided not to wait; we would go back to the church tonight.

I left Olivia a note advising her not to worry, that Eddie and I had to go out for a few hours and would be back shortly.

I decided to take the keys which opened my own tabernacle, as I had a hunch that there was a possibility the churches marked on the map would all have tabernacles, and could be accessed by the same keys... oh, my god, if only this was true! I would have in my very possession the key to the rest of the treasure!

Chapter 7

Arriving at Borro just after midnight, we decided to abandon the car in a dimly lit side street and walk slowly toward the church, taking in all around us, and making a mental note of any foreseeable obstructions. There was hardly any activity, apart from the odd stray cat. As for human life, there was none that we could see; wooden shutters were closed tight, a few still exuding dim light. The church loomed in the distance, its grandeur standing magnificent against the darkening sky. I felt the significance of what we were about to do, and wondered if we should abandon the whole idea. Eddie, on the other hand, seemed calm and resolute about the task ahead of us.

Eddie and I put on gloves, and I kept a watchful eye as Eddie produced his bag of tricks, to pick at the lock. Eddie wasn't called Nifty just because of his dress sense, but also for his adaptability in doing just this kind of underhand work. We used the back door to break in, knowing from plans we had seen of the church that this would lead us to the vestry.

We scanned the area as far as we could see and, after several minutes, acknowledged to each other with a nod that we were alone. We shone our torches around us, becoming acclimatized to our location.

The room was small in comparison to the overall building, and was used to store an abundance of robes, some possibly for the choir, others for the priest brigade. It was pitch black and the light of our torches made ghostly shadows. With pounding hearts, we moved toward the only wooden door.

I slowly turned the doorknob, and together we stepped into the dark, unoccupied church, constantly alert for any sound or indication that someone may have seen us break in. Gathering our bearings, we headed toward the altar; the scent of fresh flowers drifted aromatically before us. We edged our way toward the statues, which towered above us on hexagonal stone pedestals; Eddie stood behind the status of the Virgin Mary and I behind the statue of Jesus. We stared upward at the tabernacles.

Eddie motioned with his hand for me to come over to him, whispering: "I think we should start our work on this side first."

"Why?" I replied.

"Ladies first," Eddie shrugged.

I rolled my eyes and went along with it.

There was only one problem: the tabernacles were too high for us to reach. I was looking around for divine inspiration, when Eddie indicated for us to grab one of the pews to assist us.

Now for the moment I had been waiting for. Fumbling in my trouser pocket, I pulled out the chain with the two keys, hoping that my inkling was correct. The smaller key opened the wooden tabernacle, and sliding the base anti-clockwise inside revealed the keyhole, just as with mine. Two twists of the heavy implement, and the door swung open.

Inside was a small parcel, of nothing more than notebooks for keeping account records. I shone the torch over several pages of each notebook, which confirmed that the pads were account records, with every item listed chronologically in italic handwriting. Edie shone the torch into the opening inside the tabernacle, but there was no sign to suggest any treasures were there.

With disappointment mounting, Eddie and I carried the heavy oak bench to the other side of the altar. The sacred statue of Jesus glowed luminously in the torchlight, and I felt uncomfortable at the thought that we were about to defile the sanctity of this ancient church. We repeated the same procedure, and the door to the second tabernacle creaked open.

The disappointment at finding only a small pile of decaying

Bibles, unevenly stacked on the shelf, besieged me.

I sat on the step in front of the altar, holding my head in my hands, totally disheartened. Why was I so convinced that there would be a connection with my inherited tabernacle and the rest of the tabernacles housed in the churches?

The sound of splintering stone broke the silence.

I knew that Eddie was impulsive, but this was something else!

I lifted my head, and to my astonishment saw that Eddie was levering the inside of the tabernacle behind the statue of Jesus, in turn damaging part of the cavity walls. Absolutely flabbergasted, I walked toward Eddie in disbelief.

The base inside the tabernacle disintegrated and, with gloved hands, Eddie scooped away at the loose scraps of splintered stone and plaster. Reaching deep into the hollow, he triumphantly muttered, "Yes," holding in the air a small, dark drawstring pouch, which jingled as he shook it triumphantly. Eddie proudly stashed the pouch in the inner pocket of his leather bomber jacket and zipped it up for extra security.

I helped Eddie clean the mess as much as possible and, putting back the decaying Bibles, locked the tabernacle and hurriedly carried the pew behind the statue of Mary, where Eddie once again resumed the act of demolishing the second tabernacle interior. My heart was starting to pound; I wanted to get out as quickly as possible. At last, Eddie again victoriously whispered: "Yes!"

He passed me a silver cylindrical object, which I placed in the bag of tools.

Then, after replacing the account notepads and closing the tabernacle, we left the same way we had entered.

Once we were outside in the cool air, I inhaled and exhaled loudly, and immediately felt the tension ease from my entire body. Guilt at what we had just done weighed heavily, but the anticipation of what we would hopefully discover outweighed it more. In time, we would be making an anonymous donation to San Biagio al Borro Church in Don Pasquale Mencattini, to repent of any wrongdoing.

We arrived back in Terranuova just after four in the morning, to find Olivia already up and waiting impatiently for us to arrive. I gave her a huge hug and, without saying a word, Olivia poured three double espressos from the coffee percolator and sat beside me. "Busy night, boys?"

We both smirked. Eddie pulled out the pouch from inside his jacket pocket and poured its contents onto the kitchen table. The reflection of gold and jewels sparkled around the kitchen, creating an array of colours which swirled about the ceiling, the walls and back onto the table where they lay.

We touched and held every piece of jewellery, knowing that a small fortune was in our grasp. Eddie couldn't wait to take out his magnifying glass and study them piece by piece, to admire the clarity and craftsmanship of each individual item, and, of course, to make an overall evaluation.

Eddie finally broke the silence, whispering in utter astonishment his estimation that the items sparkling in front of us were worth a minimum of two million euros.

"Don't forget we still haven't opened the silver cylinder," I added. I removed the cylinder from the sack-cloth bag and unscrewed the top.

We were surprised to find another map and further documents written in Latin, and a gold cameo ring, which Eddie informed us would be used by cardinals and popes, to stamp their seal on important documents.

"I wonder who was the owner of this one?" Olivia mused.

I could have sat up all night staring at our discovery, but eventually I reluctantly put each item back in its case and stored them safely in the tabernacle. We must have been tired, as both Eddie and I then lay on our beds, fully clothed, and drifted off in no time.

The next day, after discussing our options concerning the new stash, we agreed that our only option was to contact Fredrik – after all, the less people we involved in this matter, the better. I was still wary of Fredrik, and even more so of his sidekick Hendrik, but I knew it was safer to sell more items to them, than to take unnecessary risks with strangers. It was also important to not stockpile our finds, but to dispose of them as soon as possible.

Eddie called Fredrik to arrange another meeting with Hendrik, and it seemed that Fredrik was every bit as interested as before in meeting with us.

We discussed the importance of not declaring our finds to the Italian treasury, in agreement that we had no choice if we wanted to get to the hidden truth. Perhaps, if our search led us to something big, we could make amends by donating a percentage back to the Italian authorities.

Olivia was more interested in the documents which had accompanied last night's find. Removing the green ribbon which held the flimsy, frayed documents together, Olivia unfolded each document carefully and laid them side by side on the coffee table, ready to begin translating them from Latin to English.

As Eddie was finalizing arrangements for our trip back to Belgium, and Olivia was studiously scribbling words on a pad from Latin to English, I seized the opportunity to cross-check the latest map we had found in the tabernacle, against the map I already had. They were works of art, decorated in an array of detail. I noticed that the town of Terranuova was marked with a gold-leafed cross, and the towns of Borro, Arezzo, Figline Valdarno and Montevarchi were marked with a water-coloured red cross; the surrounding towns had no markings at all. For a short time, everything else blended into obscurity, as I sat and admired every detail that had gone into producing what can only be described as beautiful and rare pieces of fine art.

My spellbound state was disturbed by Olivia putting a notepad under my nose and urging me to read what she had uncovered. The first line was copied word for word in Latin, *"Carus padre socerdos croci vellem, tuo gratulor laboris pecunias..."* followed by the English translation of the whole scroll:

"I would like to congratulate you on all your efforts toward the cause. The nobles of Firenze, Pisa and Arezzo, to name

but a few, are strong; however, we are still in much need for more donations. We are still in discussions with the French nobles, who will be rebelling with us, and without doubt will make us a strong force to secure our success in invading England – however, without considerable funds being added to the pot, this will remain a vision and not the reality our kindred live for. I will keep you constantly updated and informed as to our progress, and report to you when the armies are ready to march into England.

Signed,

Cardinal Bertocelli."

Eddie updated me that contact had been made with Fredrik, who had in turn contacted Hendrik, and arrangements were made to meet them this coming Friday. This gave us time to go to the next marked town on the map: Figline Valdarno, about fifteen miles south of Terranuova.

The task now facing us was to find somewhere secure to hide future treasure and such. We decided to put the money in the concealed compartment inside the tabernacle, and any treasure not yet sold in the loft, where there were a few loose bricks, which gave us the scope to hide future finds in the cavity of the wall.

Once in Figline Valdarno, we tried to find the church marked on the map. It was late in the afternoon, so we began our search by sticking to the same plan as before, working our way from the outward perimeters of the town and slowly gravitating toward the centre. I assumed the red crosses all represented churches, as the same marking had denoted the San Biagio al Borro Church, in Borro. I wondered why the churches were not marked by name; perhaps a deliberate ploy, to keep their identity a secret. I asked Olivia if there were any clues to which church it could be in the Latin writing, hoping to save some shoe leather. Unfortunately, there weren't. But, there was some good news in as much that Figline was not too vast a town in size, and therefore could not possibly have too many churches to scour.

After an hour of searching for the church, and scanning an iPad full of pictures taken for closer investigation, we had finally reached the town centre. Before any more church viewings could be made, we decided the grand piazza was an ideal place to sit for a while and mull over the snapshots, whilst enjoying long, refreshing glasses of Aperol spritz. We started looking through the photos and narrowing the churches into "possible" and "no way" categories.

Olivia and Eddie were busy discussing which churches were potential ones to revisit and which we could discard, when my eye caught sight of an official building on the far side of the piazza, approximately 400 metres away from where we were sitting. Without uttering a word, I started walking closer to the building. I was halfway across the square before I could see a bell tower, which was hidden by a tree from where we were; that was when I discovered that the building was a church and not, as I had first thought, an official establishment. The walls had a smooth, rendered finish and were painted in a non-descript muddy white. With the ornate marble pillars and a coat of arms above the entrance, the church could have easily been mistaken for an official building. The name of this unassuming church was Santa Maria.

My gut instinct told me this was "the church". There could be a pattern here; the church in Borro was also in the main square. If this was the case, our work may be easier when finding the other towns marked on the map.

I turned and walked back far enough for Olivia and Eddie to see me, and signalled with my hand for them to come over. We all walked across the square and opened the large oak door to the church.

We were obviously in need of divine intervention, as once again a service was taking place; some may even have thought this to be an omen! We sat ourselves near the exit, so as not to disturb the service.

Looking around the church, I felt the same coldness about its interior as I did about its exterior. However, when zooming in on the architecture of this humble church, I marvelled at the exquisite style used by the designer. The ornate stained-glass windows and scattered sculptured work were to be admired. To the right, there was an elaborately carved entrance, with the words *"AVE GRATIA PLENA"* written in bold letters, housing paintings and other works of art. My eyes started to scan the altar area, which was positioned two stone steps up to a balustrade, taking in as much detail as I possibly could. There was the usual layout, typical of all Catholic churches: console table with candles, and a grand, ornamental mantel, with more candles to attract the eye to the crucifix which hung in front of a row of tubular bells. The alter was framed in a semicircle, and afforded its supremacy by marble pillars on either side, stretching the height of the ceiling.

Extending my peripheral view to the side walls of the church, I could see two doors on opposing walls, facing each other: two tabernacles at the front of the church, facing the altar. As sure as one could be, I knew this was the church. I now had to work out how to gain access to them.

Remaining seated, we watched the last of the congregation finally leave, followed by the padre, who turned to us and smiled as he walked out. We heard the padre thanking folk for cleaning the church, and giving them his blessing. When we could no longer hear his footsteps, it was time for Eddie and me to go to work.

My next step was to see if old Agostino's – or, I should now say, *my* – tabernacle key would also unlock these two tabernacles. Olivia stayed seated at the back and would act as our lookout, while Eddie and I slowly walked toward the tabernacle to our left, with a quick glance to confirm that no one was around. I took the key from my pocket and, as inconspicuously as possible, slotted the key into the tabernacle's cast-iron escutcheon. To my astonishment and, of course, much disappointment, the key did not turn.

My certainty had started to become doubts about this being the right church, but I had to be sure. I walked across to check the second tabernacle. The same routine: a quick glance over my shoulder to ensure the coast was clear, before slotting the key into the keyhole.

Damn, I was wrong! I now know how Prince Charming must have felt, trying to find Cinderella.

All three of us feeling disappointed, we decided to head back to Terranuova. We were tired and hungry.

As soon as we arrived, we made our way to a restaurant called Villa Norcenni, a typical family-run establishment serving homemade cuisine. We sat ourselves around the table and made our selection from the tantalizing food on offer. The waiter smiled and recommended a bottle of Bardolino to accompany our choice of dishes.

Olivia asked if, on the way back to Terranuova from Belgium, we could take a detour to Milano. I looked at her, questioningly.

"I need to buy some clothes," she said.

Eddie laughed. "That's the spirit! You mean you need to buy some *designer* clothes! Do the shops in Terranuova not meet your requirements, then?"

We all laughed at her craftiness, but I agreed to her wishes;

she deserved to be spoilt.

Eddie then blurted out that he didn't think there was anything hidden in the tabernacles in Santa Maria at Figline, with the obvious explanation that, if there were, then the key would have opened them.

I couldn't argue with him, but asked that he remain optimistic. If the key didn't open the tabernacles, the search simply needed to continue; we just had to keep looking. The map definitely pointed to a church in Figline, indicating that we must have overlooked something.

At this point, a well-needed escape was offered by the arrival of our food. For a short while, we enjoyed making small-talk, and indulging in the feast put in front of us.

Then, with our stomachs full and our minds frazzled, we headed home, for some much-needed rest before our trip to Belgium.

Today had been a tad disappointing, but we were in it for the long haul, and had to be prepared for days like this.

Chapter 8

As soon as we got back home from the restaurant, Olivia made her excuses and made her way to the bathroom for a long soak. After a while, she came into the sitting room with her hair wrapped in a bath towel, and picked up the English newspaper she had purchased at Figline, deciding to get into bed and catch up with the news back home – I suppose once a journalist always a journalist.

While Olivia caught up with what was making headlines back in England, Eddie and I stayed up a little longer, enjoying a moment of silence whilst sipping a mug of coffee.

The phone rang and broke the silence. It was Roberto, with news regarding a flat for Eddie.

"That sounds perfect," I said. "I'll let Eddie know. When can we view it?" Eddie's ears pricked up when he realized it was Roberto ringing, to let me know about accommodation which may be suitable for him.

Roberto said that the flat belonged to a cousin of his. He went on to explain that the flat needed updating, so if Eddie was interested in carrying out the list of repairs and redecorating, he could stay there rent-free for six months, with a reasonable discount thereafter.

Eddie was over the moon. We agreed to view the flat as soon as we got back from Belgium.

The next morning, Eddie was the first up and made breakfast. Our overnight bags were already packed, so we were ready to head off to Belgium as soon as possible.

We hit the motorway and made our way up through Italy into France and Luxembourg, stopping only for a quick refreshment break, before arriving at our destination in Antwerp, Belgium.

Our reservations were already booked for the same hotel where Eddie and I stayed during our last trip here, but this time we were upgraded, as was the custom of the hotel when making a further reservation within twelve months. We wanted to provide ourselves with as much safety as possible, and asked if we could have adjoining rooms, just in case there was any trouble.

After sprucing ourselves up and changing into more suitable attire, we headed to the restaurant for a bite to eat. We resembled all the other tourists; nobody would suspect us of coming over to sell ancient jewellery. The brown holdall containing the precious stones did not leave my side, and remained positioned on the floor between my legs, as if I were guarding the Crown Jewels single-handedly.

Over dinner, Eddie discussed going back to England for a few days, before taking on his rental in Italy. He said that he would make arrangements to fit in with Olivia and me continuing our trip back to Italy; the slight change to our plan would just mean dropping Eddie off in Calais, after our trip here in Belgium. Olivia jokily asked Eddie whether her wanting to take a detour for a little retail therapy had anything to do with his decision.

We decided to have liqueur coffees delivered to Eddie's room. The waiter took our order and brought our drinks to the room, served on an ornate silver tray.

After going over the plans for the coming morning, we bade Eddie goodnight and slipped into our room via the adjoining door. We arranged for an alarm call with reception, so as not to be late for our meeting.

Fredrik must have been as anxious as we were about our meeting, as he was peering through the window when we pulled up. His eagerness gave us no doubt that he was anticipating the new set of jewels would be of the same quality and age as that he had previously purchased from us.

After the familiar shaking of hands, Fredrik led us to the back room, where Hendrik was already waiting for us. We passed on the offered refreshments, as we could sense that Fredrik's and Hendrik's body language indicated they wanted to hurry and feast on the new arrivals.

I carefully took out the jewels, piece by piece from the holdall, and placed them under their noses, knowing that they would not be disappointed. The new pieces ranged from gold coins dating back to the 16th century, to jewels encrusted with diamonds, emeralds, sapphires and rubies, to name but a few. My eyes did not move from Hendrik's face, waiting to catch any signs of astonishment, but he was a shrewd businessman and stuck to his poker face, giving no clues as to the value or quality of what lay in front of him.

After about fifteen minutes, Hendrik at last broke the silence, asking directly: "How much were you looking for?"

I knew how interested he was, and threw the question back at him: "How much are you willing to pay?"

I was not expecting anywhere near the amount that Hendrik

came out with, but I was learning fast, and kept my look of surprise to myself. I wanted Hendrik to believe that we knew the value of the jewels, and although Eddie had some idea, it was just an educated guess. So, I called his bluff by requesting that he up the price by at least a further twenty per cent, or there would be no deal. My heart was starting to beat a little faster, and I tried my hardest not to lose my cool, but it only took him three minutes to agree the price and buy the lot.

We walked out of the shop in absolute silence and, without uttering a single word, hailed a taxi to take us back to the hotel. You could have heard a pin drop for the whole journey.

Eddie paid the taxi driver and we went straight to reception, ordering two Jack Daniel's and a dry martini to be delivered to mine and Olivia's room. Olivia let us both in and gave us both a hug of relief that we were back safe. Once the drinks were delivered by room service, we sat on the bed and toasted an additional 85,000 euros!

Eddie updated Olivia with every minute detail, and how he couldn't believe that I had asked Hendrik for a further twenty per cent! My friend amused me, and made me realize how much I was enjoying getting into character. There was no one more surprised than me at how I was enjoying the thrill of our new project, and where it was leading us to.

We had enough time for a substantial lunch to celebrate the deal, before taking Eddie to Calais, to catch a ferry back to England. Eddie was going to be missed, but he had to go back and sort out his loose ends, before meeting up with us again.

Continuing through France, me and Olivia headed toward the Fréjus Tunnel taking us back to Italy, 85,000 euros better off. It was great having some time for just the two of us, and we chatted and whiled the next few hours away with idle chat and laughter.

The next stop was Milano, the city Olivia had been waiting to be unleashed on. Time dictated that, if Olivia was to enjoy her shopping spree, we would need to stay the night. Fortunately, we were not short of choice, and found a quaint hotel with only twenty rooms, pleasingly situated in the heart of the city, with car park facilities providing easy access to the abundance of shops. Olivia nodded her approval, so taking our luggage from the car, we made our way to the reception area.

Olivia was up from the crack of dawn, ready to hit the shops. I stared up at her with blurry eyes and wondered if I was going to be permitted time to get dressed! My beautiful woman looked like an excited child in a candy shop; how could I resist?

With no espresso in sight, I jumped into the shower and got dressed, Olivia waiting as patiently as she possibly could for us to get going. I handed over a bundle of notes – five-thousand euros – thinking that Olivia would say that she didn't need anywhere near that much. How wrong I was; with her beautiful mouth wide open, she thanked me, placing a kiss on my cheek, before eagerly snatching the cash and securing it in the pocket of her tight-fitted jeans. Olivia was clearly ready to shop 'til she dropped!

We went in and out of shops as if the world was going to end, and with every shop visited a little more weighed down by shopping bags. Time went into slow motion, as I felt her excitement every time she came out of a changing room, twirling to display the next purchase. I enjoyed watching her and, for a brief moment, wanted this time to last a little longer.

After hours of walking from shop to shop, I suggested a break. However, it was obvious that this notion had not even entered Olivia's head. Though, now it was suggested, she gracefully shrugged her shoulders and agreed to a break.

Finally, we were loading the car with the new purchases, checking out and heading home. It felt so good to call

Terranuova Bracciolini home! I made it crystal clear to Olivia that the money we had spent in Milano was a gift from my pocket, and was not from the proceeds of the sale of our discovered treasure.

As we got nearer to Terranuova, Olivia looked deep in thought. I knew that the same questions were running through her mind as were in mine: how was it that nobody else had discovered the jewels and maps; did anyone else discover them, and were they just waiting for the right time; what if somebody else knew that old Agostino's tabernacle key held the secrets of what had been plotted?

I knew that there had been a conspiracy – this much was confirmed in the letter sent to the cardinals, bishops and nobles of the time – but I could only come to my own conclusion as to the rest of the story. I guessed that someone within the conspiracy had got cold feet and betrayed the brothers; I would imagine that he confessed all to the pope, who in turn had all of those involved arrested and executed. But, was my imagination running away with me? Surely, this would have left alive nobody who knew where the spoils were hidden? The informer may have not known about the treasure; surely he would have talked? Perhaps each member was only given a part of the information, so that if there was a spy within the group, he would only be able to disclose a piece of the conspiracy, safeguarding as much as possible. We needed to remain alert, as the snitch who had informed the pope – or, of course, the pope himself – could have disclosed information to others; there was always the possibility that any member of the conspiracy may have passed information to a trusted friend or family member. For all I knew, Agostino may have been a descendant, and even himself known about the conspiracy. I had question after question needing answers, and I knew that the more we uncovered, every new bit of information unravelled, the more sense all of this would make.

It was then that Olivia spotted a black Mercedes following us, and gave me a nudge to look in the side mirror. I went from one lane to another, to see if they would follow and, sure as day turned to night, the car continued its pursuit; the car was following us, alright.

Confirming this was the case, and seeing there were at least two men in the car, I wanted to get home as soon as possible. I got into the fast lane and gave all the throttle the car could take. I so wished Eddie was sitting in the passenger seat, with Olivia safe back at home, but this was not the case. I wasn't going to chance Olivia getting hurt.

I spotted a road sign stating that the next services were 5km away. Thinking quickly, I took the next slip road, which led to the services.

We parked the car and made our way to the mall, seating ourselves in the most populated restaurant in the area.

Two men followed us into the restaurant and sat a few tables away from us. I told Olivia to refrain from making eye contact, and to remain as calm as possible, as I scanned the restaurant for ideas as to what to do next. There was a fire exit to our right-hand side, located next to the men's toilets.

I wanted Olivia to trust me, and tried to reassure her that we were going to be alright, as long as we remained calm. My plan was to leave Olivia at the table whilst I headed toward the men's toilets. I gave her a reassuring kiss on the cheek and walked away.

Passing the toilets, I pushed open the fire exit door and ran as fast as I could to the car park, where the black Mercedes was parked. With nothing on me to puncture the tyres, I decided to undo the dust caps and push the tyre valves as far in as they would go, using matches I thankfully carried in my pocket – this would jam the valves open and, in turn, make the tyres deflate. Taking no chances, I wedged a piece of broken bottle, lying close by, beneath one of the tyres for good measure.

With my plan put into action, I hurried back to the table and, catching the waitress's attention, ordered and paid for two espressos and a ham panini, asked for the order to be taken over to our new chums; I explained to the waitress that I had overheard them in the toilets saying they wanted to order a bite to eat, but didn't have enough money on them. I asked for my identity to remain anonymous and for her to just say it was on the house. She was impressed that someone would show such generosity, and said to leave it with her. In fact, to show unity, she would take two paninis rather than just one.

The moment the waitress walked over with the tray of unexpected goodies and began to engage the two men in conversation, I took Olivia by the hand and walked briskly out of the restaurant.

Without looking back, we drove off, leaving our new friends behind. Driving out of the restaurant, I had the vision of a comic strip running through my head: Batman and Robin getting into the batmobile and looking hastily around the car park, to see if the baddies were in pursuit, but fortunately the crooks not going anywhere fast, thanks to the quick thinking of Batman in deflating their tyres. I was enjoying my comic strip, when I caught sight of the two characters staring at the flat tyres on their vehicle, and cursing that I, Nathan Doyle – a.k.a. Batman – had outwitted them!

Now suspicion started to weigh heavily on my mind. Discounting Eddie, who had no reason to have us followed, it fell on Fredrik and that fat bastard Hendrik. By elimination, I narrowed the culprit to Hendrik; it had to be him! What was he playing at?

We managed to get back to Terranuova safely. I dropped Olivia outside the front door and passed her the numerous bags of shopping, before driving a few streets away to park the car. I walked hastily home, checking carefully that I wasn't being followed. My first thought was to call Eddie.

It was so good to hear his voice. He had only got back a few hours ago, and was surprised to hear from me so soon. We engaged in the normal polite chit-chat, establishing that his journey had been straightforward; he told me all about his connections via train from Dover to Victoria, followed by the underground straight home. He continued to tell me all about his excessive amount of mail, which needed replying to, not to mention the cheques he would have to make out to the debtors, before they sent out the firing squad. Impatiently, I cut short the small-talk and asked Eddie how soon he could return to Italy. Eddie wanted to know the reason for the urgency, and so I gave him the lowdown, from being followed by the two guys, to deflating their car tyres, to safely returning home. I went on, telling Eddie that my number one suspect was Hendrik. Eddie agreed with my train of thought and said he would tie up his business ASAP, and call me when he had booked his flight to Pisa.

As we ended the call, Olivia insisted that we needed to go food shopping, as the cupboards were bare. The risk was too high for her to go alone, so I decided to drop her off at the main shopping mall, then head over to my aunt's farm, to leave the car. The mall would be packed with people, and I knew Olivia would be safe there. I wanted the car out of sight, and knew that the farm would be the ideal place to hide it. We agreed that I would then walk back to the mall and we would get a taxi back home.

When I arrived at the farm, Aunt Marie was catching up on the local gossip with her neighbours over espresso coffees, and sweet biscuits for those not worried anymore about their figures. It was still a tad embarrassing walking toward a group of women, who as usual did nothing to hide the fact that that they were looking at me from head to toe, as if giving me a full inspection, which was customary in these parts of Italy. I nodded and smiled embarrassingly and, after the normal polite exchanges of introduction to her friends, Aunt Marie asked if I wanted to join them for coffee. Not wanting to offend the neighbourhood stronghold, I took a seat and drank coffee with these beautiful women, listening to their local gossip and wondering how they would react to what I had uncovered; how would they feel about the involvement of their ancestors in perhaps the largest conspiracy to involve the Monarchy and the Church to date?! There was the usual invasion of privacy, the ladies taking it in turn to bombard me with questions, which ranged from wanting to know if I was planning to stay and work in Italy, to asking if I was going to marry my beautiful woman friend; one lady even wanted to know if Olivia wanted children. With a smirk on my face and hints of agreement, I left the questions unanswered and let them come to their own conclusions; knowing a little about women, I felt that the blanks they filled in for themselves would be far more elaborate than any statement I could give.

I asked my aunt if it would be alright to leave the car at the farm for a few days, and made an excuse that it was the only way for me to carry out my promise to Olivia, of joining her in more walking activities, rather than driving everywhere. I went on to jokingly say that I was weak and needed to avoid temptation. Laughing at me, she nodded and added how it always took a woman to encourage the males to lead a healthier lifestyle.

I shrugged my shoulders and then kissed her goodbye, waving to my new friends, who insisted I join them for coffee soon, and next time to bring Olivia – most probably to extract more information.

By the time I got back to the shopping mall, Olivia was already standing there waiting for me, with three bulging shopping bags. We hailed a taxi to take us home.

Once back in Terranuova, because it was late and neither of us wanted to take the time to cook a proper meal, we prepared a tapas-style buffet, which we enjoyed with a glass of rich red Chianti.

We made a decision that the Mini Cooper had to go, to buy time from whoever was following us. I called Roberto and asked if there was anything in his garage to upgrade the Mini, as we wanted a car with a little more room. Roberto's garage was only a small concern, and he informed me that he didn't have anything suitable, but he was happy to take back the Mini Cooper, as he would have no problem selling it on. As the car was already at Auntie Marie's, I said I would meet him at his garage to drop off the keys.

"I also have the keys to my cousin's flat," he told me. "Shall I bring them so Eddie can view it?"

I replied: "Sounds good to me. We'll see you tomorrow."

Roberto added: "Nathan, remember your cousin Marco?"

"Yes, of course I do."

"If it's a quality car you are looking for, go see your cousin in Montevarchi."

Chapter 9

With no transport, we headed to the bus stop which would take us to Montevarchi, only a short ride away. My cousin Marco who, for several reasons, I hadn't seen for about three years, owned a car showroom, amongst other enterprises; I knew he would have a car that would suit our needs.

He was chatting to a customer when we arrived, so I stood about five yards away from him and waited. He turned in my direction at least four or five times, before making a gesture that someone would be with us shortly.

I nodded and called out: "No problem."

Marco looked over at me once again, this time looking slightly puzzled, before breaking into a smile, indicating that at last he recognized me. Letting his customer browse, he walked over and put one hand in the palm of mine and the other on my shoulder, greeting me with his infamous words: "How are you, English man? How long are you staying this time?"

I waved circles in the air, as if to say for a long time. I turned toward Olivia to introduce her to Marco, but only got as far as her name before he took over the introductions with his broken English, at the same time taking her hand and planting a seductive kiss, while not allowing his eyes to lose contact with hers. Very smooth. I could see Olivia smirking at Marco's stereotypical innuendos, and before his flirting became too embarrassing, I intervened by asking after the family.

Soon back to business, I explained that I was looking for a good, reliable car with a little style.

With a big grin on his face, Marco replied: "I have just the car for you, cousin. Come and see for yourself." He walked us over to a black Alfa Romeo Brera and, with Italian passion for the model, began to give us the full lowdown on the car. Marco described the car's looks as if describing a lover, before adding commentary on the car's impressive 200kph performance capacity. He continued to describe the luxurious leather interior, whilst running his fingers across one of the seats, and with enthusiasm informed us that it also had the added specification of black tinted windows – a must, he went on to say, in hot countries. Oh, Marco, the sun was the least of my concerns, but I humoured him with the appropriate *hmms* and *wows* to show my appreciation.

"It's *beni beni*, huh? Do you like? I can give you a good

discount – after all, you are family." Marco rubbed his chin, before adding that for 18,000 euros it could be mine. I stayed quiet and, after a short silence, Marco asked if I was paying in cash; if so, he would accept 14,000 euros today, or tomorrow at the latest. We shook on the deal and made arrangements for me to come back with the money the next day.

After more kisses for Olivia, and the normal farewells for me, we waved Marco goodbye. Marco insisted that we visit him at his home soon; he would get Antonella (yes, Marco was married) to cook a typical Italian dish for us. We assured him that we would take him up on his kind offer, and in my head I knew that this would be happening sooner than he was thinking. I had known that Marco had a car showroom in Montevarchi, even before Roberto had mentioned it to me, but my business with Marco was not just for a car. He insisted that one of his staff take us back to Terranuova and, not wanting to appear ungrateful, we thanked him for his hospitality and accepted the lift.

Later that evening, I made my excuses to Olivia, and said that I needed to go for a walk, so I could walk off the scrumptious dinner she had cooked for us. But I was fooling nobody; Olivia knew me well enough to know that my best problem-solving was resolved in solitude. I reassured her that I wouldn't be too long.

I wanted to pay Marco a visit at his home alone, and took the short taxi drive to his house. When I arrived, Marco was playing in the front garden with his German shepherd dog. His villa was as grand as any other located in this popular part of town, and the prestige of owning property here suited Marco's ego. I opened the gate and started to approach him, as his obedient dog let him know that he had a visitor. Marco turned to see why Marco Junior (only Marco would name his dog after himself) was barking; once he saw that it was me, he signalled his mutt to stop his barking.

"Salve, Nathan. How is my friend?"

I replied that I was very well and, after the pleasantries, was led inside to meet Antonella and the family. Being typically Mediterranean, Marco asked if I had eaten, before accepting that a cold drink was all I wanted. Antonella hurried into the kitchen and returned with two tall glasses of chilled pink lemonade, with crushed strawberries and a sprig of mint for added flavour, and left us men to catch up with each other's news. Marco sensed that my visit was more than just a social one, and asked directly if everything was okay.

“Marco, I need a gun. A hand pistol.”

He looked concerned, and wanted to know why I would need a pistol – especially here in Italy. I tried to reassure him that it was only for security and most probably wouldn’t be needed at all. “Marco I’ve been doing some business with a couple of guys in Belgium; on my last return trip home I was followed. I managed to lose them, but I suspect they are linked to the men I’m doing business with out there. I can’t tell you any more at this present time; I just ask that you believe I wouldn’t be involved in anything illegal. What I have found myself caught up in needs time for me to uncover all the pieces of the jigsaw puzzle, and I know it will be for a good cause – unfortunately, there may be obstacles to deal with on the way. That’s why I need the pistol. It is no more than a backup, and only then as a last resort, if things turn nasty.”

Marco looked at me understandingly, and wanted to know how he could help. At the very least, he wanted to arrange for one of his associates to accompany me as protection.

I explained that this was not necessary, as I had a trusted friend who would be with me for as long as it took for my project to be completed. With a concerned and hesitant nod, Marco conceded to the fact that, other than the gun, no other help was required.

"Nathan, the pistol will be with you in twenty-four hours. I just hope you know what you are doing."

I reassured him that I had everything under control and thanked him.

Although we already had arrangements for me to pick up the car at midday, we arranged to meet the following evening at eight p.m. in the piazza, at a small coffee shop, regarding the pistol.

Marco then called out to Antonella to come and say ciao, but she was busy putting the children to bed. I called out for her not to worry, and that next time I would come earlier and bring my ladyfriend with me, joking about wanting her endorsement of my choice for a partner. Antonella laughed and said that she would look forward to seeing my ladyfriend – but not for the reason I had asked; on the contrary, it was to see if *I* was worthy of the girl! I laughed and once again thanked Marco for his assistance in my little problem. Marco then drove me home, now a little less worried.

I arrived back just in time to join Olivia in a glass of red wine. I mentioned that I had taken a detour and visited Marco and his family, but left out the details of arranging to pick up a pistol from him tomorrow evening. I could see from Olivia's face that she was a little disappointed that I didn't ask her to join me, so I went on to explain that it was not a planned visit, and that I had promised Marco and Antonella I would be back for a longer visit with my beautiful Olivia, as I wanted Antonella to meet her. She grinned, satisfied with my reassurance that she was included in my plans.

I informed her that the Alfa was going to be ready by lunchtime tomorrow. Olivia was glad about this, and wanted to know if there was time for a small trip to Pompeii, to do some sightseeing before business matters resumed. There was a small silence, before I informed her that Eddie had called to say he was returning tomorrow, so after picking up the Alfa I was going to collect Eddie from Pisa airport, then the two of us had some business with Marco at eight o'clock. "Then I want me and Eddie to take a trip back to Belgium, the day after tomorrow."

Olivia looked at me a little confused, and said: "I didn't think you had anything else to sell. So, why the trip?"

I tried to explain that if there were to be further exchanges between us and the two Belgians, I needed to establish that they could uphold their part of the business.

"Okay, I get it. I suppose I can continue my research while you two play diamond merchants."

The next morning, after a light breakfast of croissants and coffee, we made our way to Montevarchi to collect the car.

I walked into the office to complete the paperwork and pay the 14,000 euros. I had divided the money into fourteen separate bundles, which I handed to Marco after receiving the car's service history, test certificate and logbook.

Marco then handed over a plastic carrier bag and added: "The package we discussed last night." He went on to explain that his contacts already had what I was looking for "in stock", adding that he didn't want any money, and I should treat it as a gift. We shook hands.

Realizing I was now holding a pistol in my hand, I struggled desperately not to feel like I looked suspicious. Thankfully, the car was only a stone's throw away from the reception area. I walked toward it, opened the boot and placed the pistol under the mat, concealing it between the spare tyre and wall for safekeeping.

Before going to the airport to collect Eddie, Olivia and I took time out to visit Roberto; it was a pleasant distraction from the "project".

I then dropped Olivia off before making my way to Pisa airport.

Chapter 10

Eddie looked pleased to be back. He put his suitcase in the boot and the rest of his belongings on the back seat, and praised me for my excellent choice of car. Eddie then joked that he was starving, and wanted to know what we had cooked for the return of a prodigal friend.

I laughed and said: “From the amount of food she bought, I’m sure Olivia will do you proud.”

We spent the hours driving home catching up with the everyday updates, before I informed Eddie what I had planned.

“I feel it is best we confront them sooner rather than later. I know that whoever followed us home must be connected to either Hendrik or Fredrik, or both.”

After a thoughtful silence, Eddie stated: “I hope it’s not Fredrik.”

It was good to have Eddie back, to discuss matters that I didn’t want Olivia concerned with. I was even more reassured when Eddie added: “I agree; the sooner we go and see them, the better.”

We were soon back in Terranuova.

"I have another surprise for you," I added, as we pulled up: "welcome to your new abode."

Eddie grinned in astonishment. "You mean I'm practically just across the road from you?!"

"Yep, it's the flat above the café," I replied. "Needs some T.L.C., but I know you can make it a cool pad."

Eddie seemed excited, and we wasted no time calling Roberto, to say that Eddie would be moving in by the end of the week.

Olivia cooked a typical Italian meal for the return of our good friend, proudly parading her homemade lasagne under our noses. She continued, in a theatrical silver-server stance, to promote her food by telling us that the scrumptious lasagne would be accompanied by a green salad using only the freshest local produce, lightly tossed in balsamic vinaigrette, and washed down with a bottle of Barolo red wine. We laughed and joined her at the dinner table which, added to the fine cuisine, was laden with side plates for our hot, crusty garlic rolls, and decorated with napkins and even a lit candle for atmosphere.

After much small-talk and compliment to the chef, I brought the conversation back to Figlini and the Santa Maria church; although the key did not fit the tabernacles, I was still convinced that it was the right place.

Eddie fetched the photos that Olivia had taken of the tabernacles, and we all became engrossed in them, studying to see if we had missed anything.

Was it my imagination, or were the escutcheons therein unlike others used in the 16th century? I grabbed the magnifying glass for a closer inspection, and could confirm that the escutcheons were indeed brass, rather than cast iron. It also became clear to me that the locks were of a later date. It therefore followed that my key may have fitted the original locks. I still believed, however, that once inside the tabernacles, the larger key would open the inner shelf. There was only one way to find out: we would need to break in and force the locks.

That night brought its own trail of thoughts, my mind primarily occupied by how we were going to handle Hendrik and/ or Fredrik, and the two merry men who had followed us.

What was happening to my life? The last few months had been a major rollercoaster, the twists unpredictable, the excitement riveting and the new lifestyle unbelievable. Who would believe that I would now be in possession of a pistol, stashed in a car purchased less than twenty-four hours ago? I, Nathan Doyle, could be a cast member in the next sequel to *The*

Godfather!

*

The next morning, we were ready for our trip back to Belgium.

Chapter 11

We soon hit the motorway for our trip back to Belgium – only this time not to sell, but to find out what was going on.

Getting the new car gave me the excuse to open up for a real test drive, and with a quick glance at Eddie, I warned: "Settle back and enjoy the ride." I then took to the fast lane and gave the throttle a little more, then a little more, until it felt like we were flying! At 230kph I knew the car still had more to give, but I also knew that I needed to slow down, before the polizei were on my back.

Eddie screeched: "You're like a kid with a new toy! Stop drawing attention to us!" Eddie was relieved when the speed was dropped to a steadier pace.

"What are your plans when this is all over?" he asked inquisitively, continuing without waiting for an answer. "Have you thought about maybe getting married? Maybe some offspring of your own? Buy a villa in Terranuova and settle down to marital bliss?"

I took a while to answer. After mulling the idea over, I

glanced over at him and said: “I might write a book. After all, what we are discovering is pretty important and deserves to be accurately documented. Who better to do that than the people who uncovered it?”

I then asked Eddie the same question, a little concerned at what his response might be. But I was pleasantly surprised. Eddie had already lived with a couple of his conquests in the past, and even took the plunge to marry once. Yet, he still seemed to want to meet a girl, fall madly in love and settle down again. He went on to add that perhaps he would stay permanently in Italy, and be my neighbour.

This amused me; life with Eddie as a neighbour would be anything but dull. I joked that maybe he should chat up some of the Italian bellas – though he might benefit from taking Italian lessons first, or they would struggle to communicate!

Eddie laughed and said: “We might get on better if we don’t understand what the other is saying.”

“So, do you want me to speak to Fredrik?” Eddie asked. “After all, he is supposed to be a friend of mine.”

“When we get to Fredrik’s shop, I don’t want to beat around

the bush, Eddie; I will ask him, straight to the point, why they had us followed. I want to know what's occurring. With this in mind, Eddie, I need you to trust me and do as I say."

Without any hesitation, Eddie nodded, signalling that this was fine with him.

I continued: "But, as Fredrik's your friend, can you call him when we reach the hotel and tell him that we are in Antwerp? Ask him if we can meet with him and Hendrik at ten a.m. Just say that we've got something interesting to show him."

Eddie nodded, again not questioning my intentions.

With no prebooked hotel, we took a chance on Hotel Mondo Eden Antwerpen. From the outside it looked like a modern city hotel. Its location was perfectly situated in the diamond district, so not far from Fredrik's shop, and the added advantage was that the hotel had underground car parking, which more than made up for its basic decor. Our room was clean and adequate for a night's stay. The hotel did not have a bar or restaurant, but the room included breakfast.

Eddie wasted no time contacting Fredrik and, after some basic niceties, made arrangements for us to meet him and Hendrik the next morning, at ten o'clock.

Then, both feeling pretty tired, we decided to have a bite at the nearest restaurant to the hotel, before heading back for an early night.

The adrenalin kicked in the moment I got up.

I parked the car a few roads away and we walked toward the jewellery shop, noticing every passer-by, just in case we were being followed. Strangely, the shop still had its *"Closed"* sign showing, which we were not expecting, so I rang the bell cautiously.

Fredrik opened the door and, with no more than a nod, we followed him to the back room. My hand was in my pocket, my fingers wrapped around the pistol, ready for any incident.

Hendrik was already waiting for us, and got up as soon as we entered the room, to welcome us back. After some polite banter, Hendrik could then no longer contain his eagerness, and blurted out: "After your call last night, I could hardly sleep from curiosity as to what you might be bringing us. My inquisitiveness can't wait any longer; please, end my suspense and show me what you've brought for us today."

I said: "This time it's more about what you can do for us." Seeing the puzzled look on his face, I continued: "Why did you have us followed?"

He looked puzzled and squirmed. "What are you talking about, Nathan?"

I answered within a millisecond: "I think you know exactly what I'm talking about. Until this is resolved, you will see no more of the precious jewels we can supply you with."

At that moment, I took out the pistol and held it to his head.

Both Eddie and Fredrik looked shocked, as Hendrik started to change colour, perspiring profusely, his hands shaking. I looked over at Eddie and could see that he too was sweating.

Hendrik piped up, saying: "Okay, I admit I had you followed! Please, put the gun down! I just wanted to know where you were getting such rare pieces from."

I prodded the gun deeper into his temple, adding: "Did your plans include having us killed? How greedy can one man be? Did you think I would be stupid enough to let you know where our jewels can be found?"

"Please, I can't talk with a gun pointing at my head. Please put the gun down and I'll answer all your questions."

I took five steps back – just enough to still have control of the situation, with enough space between us to allow him to breathe a little easier.

He assured me that murder was not his plan; he was just curious to know who my supplier was. He went on to say that this would make no difference to his interest in the items; curiosity took over, that was all.

"If that is the case, get your friends on the phone now and tell them their services are no longer required."

Without any hesitation, Fredrik passed the phone over to Hendrik, who immediately started dialling. When the call was connected, we heard him give strict instructions that we were not to be followed anymore.

I warned him that this scenario had better not happen again, or next time his brains would be all over the floor. He reassured me that there would be no more issues of trust, and hoped that this would not prevent me from continuing to do business with him. Then we left the shop in silence.

Eddie still looked shocked, so I placed a hand on his shoulder, to reassure him that everything was under control again. "Sorry, mate. I didn't mean to frighten you, but it had to be done. Are you okay?"

"I thought you were going to blow his fucking head off! I've never seen you looking so dangerous; it was like you were auditioning for a part in some Mafia gangster movie. Is that gun real? What have you become?" I could feel Eddie's distress at what had just happened.

"Eddie, I genuinely thought that Olivia and I were going to be murdered; I won't take any chances with our lives. I can assure you that I am still the same person you know, but it is important that Fredrik and Hendrik know not to mess with us, otherwise our lives may be put in danger."

After an uncomfortable silence, Eddie spoke: "So, who provided the shooter?" Before I could answer, he added: "Actually, don't tell me; I don't need to know."

Both me and Eddie wanted to get back to Terranuova as soon as possible. So, without any hesitation, we packed our bags, settled our tab and made tracks, only stopping to make a quick call to Olivia, to say that we were on our way home and all was well.

We got onto the German autobahn, where there is no speeding restriction, giving me an excuse to test how much power the Alfa had; hitting the accelerator to full throttle, we reached 200kph in no time.

Checking my mirror constantly, I noticed another Alfa G.T. keeping pace with me. At first I thought it was just another car enthusiast, testing his car's performance capability; then I noticed that every time I slowed down, he did, too, and every time I changed lanes, so did he. I was beginning to feel a little sense of déjà vu. Was Hendrik really so stupid as to continue his silly games?

Once the road in front of me cleared, I stepped hard on the throttle and took the next exit off of the autobahn; the red Alfa continued its pursuit. I asked Eddie to reach over and get the gun out of my jacket pocket.

Sensing Eddie's unease, I added: "I know you don't feel comfortable, but it looks like this trip isn't panning out as expected. So, just in case things get a little scary, the gun is for our protection and will only be used if we are forced to." Eddie did as I asked, removing the gun from my jacket, and placed it in my lap.

I could see a sign advertising a local restaurant, so I decided to make this our stop. Leaving nothing to chance, I parked the car as near to the restaurant's entrance as was permitted, and told Eddie, on the count of three, to open the door and head straight into the restaurant.

Once inside, we picked a table by the window, peering through the voile net certain. We watched as the red Alfa pulled into the car park, drove past our car and parked about fifty metres away from it.

We decided to order a light lunch, as we felt that nothing was going to happen to us inside the restaurant. This would also give us some time to think about what we were going to do next.

"Nathan, it doesn't make sense; Fredrik and Hendrik know that we are carrying no jewels or money, as there was no transaction between us. Why would they risk us not doing business with them anymore?" Eddie was right: it wasn't making sense.

I pretended to use the facilities, and took a diversion out of the restaurant and over to the red Alfa.

Two men were sitting in the car, one eating what looked like a sausage roll whilst talking on his mobile, the other reading a newspaper. Without being seen, I walked around the car and hid behind a small tree on the walkway, close enough to notice that the car had Italian number plates with the area code A, meaning the car was registered in Arezzo.

I made my way back inside the restaurant and let Eddie know.

He responded: "I can't see Fredrik or Hendrik hiring people from Arezzo to have us followed – that would be stupid."

Then, it dawned on me: the only other person who knew I was in some sort of situation was Marco. I picked up my phone and started dialling.

"Hello, my English friend. Have I offended you in any way? I know from this call that you have worked it out; the two not so good-looking men inside the red Alfa are my friends. Nathan, we are blood relatives. I am not suggesting that you are not capable of taking care of yourself; I just wanted to stack the odds in your favour, to make sure nothing bad was going to happen to my cousin. Do you forgive me?"

We laughed a little, and I thanked him for his genuine concern for our welfare. Marco said that he would call his friends back home. On our way back to the car, they waved to us in confirmation that their services were not needed.

The journey back to Terranuova was thereafter quiet, with the occasional reference to our friends in the red Alfa. Eddie was relieved, as I was, that the gun was safely back in my jacket pocket.

It took a further six hours to get home, and we arrived early in the evening. From the expression on Olivia's face, it was clear to see that she was pleased to see us. I scooped her in my arms and gave her a lingering kiss, which let her know that I had missed her, too.

Olivia poured us a glass of pink lemonade and warmed up croissants, then sat down, commanding that we tell her in detail about the confrontational meeting with our Belgian acquaintances.

Once Olivia was up to speed with chapter and verse, we decided to call it a night; the long journey and ongoing adrenaline rush had taken its toll. Eddie decided to head across the road to his flat, a day earlier than expected.

"Are you sure, mate? You can always go in the morning."

Eddie nodded and said: "I know I can, but I feel like a bit of a gooseberry; I'll let you lovebirds have some time alone."

Watching Eddie walk across the square from the sitting room window, I jokily called out: "Miss you already!"

The next morning, I was up early. I left Olivia a note explaining that I was going to see Marco, and should only be gone for about an hour.

Marco welcomed me with his normal charm and, clasping his face in his hands, went on to say: "Do you forgive me, cousin? I only wanted to help."

I knew Marco's actions were only made out of concern for my welfare, but I would have preferred to know about additional bodyguards on my trip. Marco interrupted my protestations by saying:

"Come on, cousin. If I told you what I was doing, you would have said no. It was more important to look out for you than worry about the small risk you might be a little annoyed with me."

I reassured Marco that I was touched by his concerns and I understood; I would most probably have done the same if the circumstances were reversed.

Once the air was cleared, Marco took the opportunity to invite all of us over for Sunday lunch, adding that Antonella was eager to meet Olivia. I knew that we had no other plans, and that Olivia would be equally eager to meet my family, so I accepted his generous invitation.

"Bring your friend, too."

I nodded and slapped him on the back, thanking him for what he had done for me.

I was a little longer than anticipated, so on the way home I called Olivia; "Hello, darling. Sorry, I've been gone longer than I anticipated. How about meeting me at Mario's pizza house for lunch?"

"Shall we see if Eddie wants to join us?" Olivia replied.

"Okay, I'll ring him."

I got to Mario's pizza house before Eddie and Olivia, and was sipping a cold glass of lager and lemonade, when I caught sight of my friend and Olivia laughing and chatting together, whilst walking toward me. I was so glad that they had hit it off.

We ordered pizzas with a variety of toppings, prepared and cooked in wood-fired ovens, enhancing both the taste and the aroma, bringing all one's senses into play. I passed onto them Marco's invitation for lunch this coming Sunday, and got two yesses – Eddie because he enjoyed good food, and Olivia because, as I knew, she wanted to meet more family members. Then came the Spanish Inquisition: Olivia wanted to know all about Marco's family before our visit.

I began by giving an outline of the family connection between Marco and myself, explaining that Marco's father Aldo was my mother's older brother. He was quite a character, and from whom I was sure that Marco got his sense of humour. Aldo owned a construction company, and the story goes that he bribed every person who worked at the council, including the mayor, to gain influence and many large contracts. When he died, he left a handsome fortune to the family, with Marco the main benefactor. Marco, in turn, carried on with his father's construction business, whilst adding to his empire other moneymaking interests, one being the car sales forecourt. Because of his father's connections, Marco was very well respected throughout Tuscany.

Olivia wanted to know if Marco had connections to the Mafia, a subject I knew little about. I only knew that nobody in their right mind would cross him, as he had connections throughout Tuscany and other parts of Italy. Olivia continued her line of questions, wanting to know how Marco met Antonella; whether it was an arranged marriage, or if he had chosen for himself that she was to be his bride. I jokingly said that this was an area I had no knowledge about; perhaps it could be the icebreaker topic of conversation, when she met Antonella on Sunday.

Olivia wanted to find a hair salon, as she'd not had a haircut since her last visit to London. Eddie was commencing decorating the flat, so I took the opportunity to research history of the Church and the Monarchy dating back to the 1530s. It was a welcome chance to educate myself in early English and Italian history.

My time was rewarded with useful information and stories

about the reformation years. I connected the printer to the P.C. and printed relevant pieces, which might help with uncovering the secrets of our found treasure and accompanying documents.

One documented article covered the reformation years, between King Francis I of France and King Henry VIII of England; it outlined how Francis was a staunch Catholic, known as one of the pillars of the Roman Catholic Church, continuing with how he was under pressure from his nobles to participate in a crusade against Henry, following the insults Rome had suffered whilst he was in power. A *Bill of Deprivation*, first drafted in 1535, called on all Christians to attack and destroy the English Monarchy. I didn't need to be Einstein to know that the attack and usurping of Henry VIII did not take place, so I could only assume that the pope did not give his support to the campaign.

My thoughts perplexed me, so I took a break and made coffee, before continuing my search for answers. I wondered if the cardinals and bishops supporting Francis had formed a conspiracy against the pope, gaining support from the nobles of Italy and France. Did they continue to plot against the Monarchy without the pope's knowledge? And, if so, where was the money coming from to fund this war? With the evidence of the treasures in my possession, and of course the letter Olivia had managed to translate from Cardinal Bertocelli, I now felt strongly that a conspiracy had been formed.

The pope had spies working for him at home and abroad, and would surely have been informed that a conspiracy was developing within the Vatican, which he clearly was not part of. Once this was brought to his attention, he must have felt that this action would have serious repercussions and decreed to have all concerned executed.

The treasures curated to fund this attack may have remained unknown forever, had I not moved into Agostino's property. I felt like a disciple, chosen to bring the truth to the people. I, Nathan Doyle, a run-of-the-mill guy, had been adorned with this incredible honour of uncovering a part of history – a conspiracy against the king of England, no less!

Olivia was delighted that the hairdresser had styled her hair just as well as they did in London, at a fraction of the price, joking that she would treat me to an ice cream with her savings. It was wonderful strolling hand in hand, eating gelatos and feeling the warm sun on our skin.

On our way back, we paid Eddie a visit. He was still busy

preparing the walls for the new paint he had bought. We convinced him to take a break and join us in the café for refreshments, where Eddie complimented Olivia on her hair and asked me what I'd been up to.

"I've been doing a little research into history around the 1530s."

They both listened attentively. Once they knew as much as I did, Eddie said: "If this is true, it means that there will be treasure stashed in numerous places all over Italy. It may take us a lifetime to discover it!"

I simply replied: "But, what a hobby to have."

Chapter 12

Sunday soon came around, and we were on our way to keep our rendezvous with Marco and his family. Olivia decided to purchase a small bouquet of flowers for Antonetta, chocolates for the children and a cigar for Marco. Another reason why I loved her: Olivia had always been thoughtful, and it made me feel happy that she wanted to make a good impression when meeting others. Eddie decided a bottle of Chianti and an assortment of miniature cakes, carefully packed in a white cardboard box, was the perfect offering.

Antonella saw us walking toward the house, and started down the path to greet us, with a welcoming smile. I introduced her to Olivia, and with broken English Antonella thanked Olivia for the flowers, signalling to follow her into the kitchen. The children were summoned to show off the basic English they had learnt from their private English tutor, and Olivia showed her appreciation by greeting them back with the few Italian words she had been practicing.

The afternoon passed so quickly and, after taking a further

twenty minutes or so to say our goodbyes, we were already making our way back home. It was great to relax and enjoy some sense of normality; a much welcome diversion from the antics of the last few days. Tomorrow we would get back to business.

Olivia decided that, to help us put the pieces together, we needed to go farther back in time; her hunch was that we needed to understand more about the laws and cultural background of Terranuova, and the areas in its close proximity. She wanted to compile a record of events which, in turn, might help to identify new leads. "Whatever you already know, darling, will be my starting point."

"Okay," I said, thoughtfully, "I know that the town's name originated from a guy called Gian Francesco Poggio Bracciolini, and that he was born in Terranuova in 1380, and died in 1459."

"Well, that's a start. I'll see what else I can find on our man."

I made us coffee, then, as promised, went over to give Eddie a hand redecorating his new home.

Meanwhile, Olivia went on to discover that Poggio Bracciolini, as he was known back in the day, was an Italian scholar and a humanist; it was whilst working in Florence, as a copyist of manuscripts, that he invented the humanist script: some type of formal writing which, after years of polishing by engravers, became the prototype of the Roman fonts. In 1403 he moved to Rome, where he became secretary to Pope Boniface IX. He actually spent four years in England, but was disappointed by the inadequacies of the English libraries, and so returned to Rome in 1423, where he was reappointed curial secretary. He was the man responsible for rediscovering and recovering a great number of classical Latin manuscripts.

Because of Poggio Bracciolini's position, he was held in high esteem by the public, and when he wanted to marry an eighteen-year-old daughter of a high-ranking Florentine noble, the family treated his bequest as an honour. The people of the town honoured this fascinating man by naming the town after him, in recognition of his achievements as an Italian humanist and a master calligrapher.

"Hi, darling. Are you and Eddie enjoying painting walls?"

"I wouldn't go that far, but I suppose it's artistic. I know it's made us hungry."

"Is that a hint?"

"Well, if that's okay with you?" We laughed and agreed to come back over in half an hour.

Olivia cut bread, tomatoes, olives, mozzarella, prosciutto and lettuce. We had definitely acclimatized to the Italian way of living.

Olivia updated us on Terranuova's famous son, adding: "Do you think it's coincidental that the first scrolls were discovered here, in the town named after the inventor of script-writing – a copyist of manuscripts – not to mention being connected to popes and mingling with nobles of that time?"

"This all happened before the period in question. Are we not overthinking the plot? I suppose we can keep the notes and see if we discover anything to link him to what we have uncovered so far."

We arranged to revisit the church in Figline, agreeing to leave Terranuova early the next morning. Eddie then went back to his place, and I took the time to look over the notes on Signor Bracciolini.

My mind turned back to Agostino. He had to have a connection to the plot. "Olivia, I think we need to dig into Agostino's past."

Olivia responded: "I was thinking that, too."

The next morning, we made our way back to Figline, with a small matter to work out: how we were going to open the tabernacles in Santa Maria Church, without access to the new key.

Eddie scanned the perimeter of the church, whilst Olivia and I posed as tourists, who were simply admiring the artwork and ornate holy statues. There were a few lost souls finding solace in sitting quietly with their thoughts, and others kneeling, praying to their God. I could see no alternative, other than to break into yet another church. Then Eddie walked over and whispered that he had a plan.

We followed him out of the church and sat in a nearby café, eager to hear what Eddie's plan was. He could hardly wait to share his lightbulb moment with us, and started with the words: "You two are getting married. You need to make an appointment to discuss available dates with the father."

This took both of us by surprise; how was this helping with access to the tabernacles?

My friend went on to explain that, for sure, the key would be kept in the vestry, and what better way to gain access to the room than posing as a loving couple who wished to be wed in this beautiful church?

Olivia and I looked at him, both wanting to know how this was going to help us gain possession of the key.

"Ah, well, while you two make the arrangements for your coming wedding, I – the best man – will be accompanying you, and I will use the opportunity to scour the room for the key. The codeword will be *'Alright for me to wait for you outside?'* – if I say that, then you will know I have managed to locate the key."

"Won't they miss the key?" Olivia asked.

"The key will be returned as soon as I have taken a copy of it; no one will know it ever left the building."

We were actually impressed with Eddie's idea. However, there was still the small matter of how we were going to get into the church in the first place. But, it seemed that Eddie was one step ahead of us; whilst perusing the exterior, he noticed that there was a weakness in one of the windows to the right-hand side of the church, which could easily be removed and put back when our work was completed. Eddie felt so pleased with himself; it was obvious that the adventure made him feel exhilarated.

But it bothered me to give a locksmith a mould of the tabernacle key. What if he thought it suspicious? I asked Eddie if the idea could be dropped. "Eddie, let's not over-complicate the matter of the key. I don't think it will be a problem to just 'borrow' it for the day, then put it back. No one else will suspect us of foul play."

Eddie nodded and replied: "Yep, I suppose you're right; I think I was getting carried away. We'll take it with us and put it back on our way out."

Olivia left us to go and find a contact number for the priest. She came back shortly with a young lady, who informed us that the priest always went to the local hospital at lunchtime, to pray with relatives who had lost loved ones, and any other pastoral duties; she informed us that he should be back around three p.m. The young lady worked as a volunteer at the church three times a week, and told us that this was Father Patrizzio's daily routine. So, with less than half an hour to wait, we decided to enjoy a stroll, admiring the beautiful architecture of the town.

As soon as we caught sight of Father Patrizzio heading toward the church, we were quick to catch him up and put our request to him. Olivia looked at him anxiously, and used her persuasive way to get the priest to agree to seeing us straight away. My Olivia seemed to have a way about her that even a man of the cloth could not say no to!

As the four of us went into the vestry, the father looked over at Eddie inquisitively, as if to establish his purpose or involvement in this situation. I introduced Eddie as my best man, and asked if it would be okay for him to join us. Thank goodness he said yes, and the plan commenced.

The priest took charge by asking numerous questions, for which, I hasten to add, neither of us were prepared; we hoped that Eddie wasn't going to take too long finding the relevant key. It was as if we were performing in some romantic film – and I could see that Olivia was really getting into character.

Eddie then signalled to ask if it was okay for him to wait outside, and I knew this meant that he had retrieved the key.

It became clear, from the line of questioning, that it would not be possible for us to reserve a wedding date, until we had satisfied the priest with relevant documentation, such as our freedom papers and proof of who we were. So, we thanked him for his time and took the leaflet with his contact telephone number, to call him should we wish to go ahead.

Back home in Terranuova, my and Eddie's thoughts were focused on our next visit to Santa Maria. Olivia began gathering information on Agostino's ancestors but, as it was late, the offices holding records for these matters were closed, and so matters would have to wait until tomorrow.

That night, Olivia was quieter than normal, and I asked her if she was okay. In typical female style, she responded that she was okay, which I knew was a load of baloney. But, in typical male style, I thought it best not to probe for information, so just lay silently beside her.

"I enjoyed today, visiting Father Patrizzio. I suppose that's what it feels like when a couple take the next step in their relationship, making that commitment to each other by exchanging wedding vows," she said.

With no further conversation, I kissed her and held her closer to me. I felt a closeness between us, as if we had already silently made our vows to one another.

The next morning, I dropped Olivia at the registrar's office, so that she could gather information on Agostino, whilst I went round to help Eddie with some decorating and to mull over the plan for tonight.

The day went by so quickly, and before long I left Eddie to get ready for tonight's outing.

Olivia was already home when I got back, and couldn't wait to share the news of what she had discovered.

"Okay," she began, as she made herself comfortable in the armchair by the window, "this house has belonged to Agostino Mancini's family for over two hundred years. Years ago, the place was a Franciscan monastery, where monks would gather for prayers and bless the holy water, which I assume was kept in the tabernacle. Your Nono Agostino was born in 1930; his father's date of birth was 1895; his grandfather's date of birth was 1877; and his great grandfather, named Giuseppe Mancini, was born in 1831. I traced a further two great, great grandfathers, who were born in 1797 and 1773.

"This is where it gets interesting. Agostino's great, great, great, great, great grandfather was actually born in Rome. His name was Francesco Mancini, and he held the position of Captain of the Guard in – wait for it – the Vatican!

"There was a fire in Rome, which caused many building to be destroyed, including the town hall, where many documents were lost. But at some point Francesco Mancini came back to Arezzo, because this is where he died."

Olivia now had my undivided attention, and she continued:

"Could Francesco have stumbled across the documents relating to Cardinal Bertocelli? He comes back to Arezzo Terranuova, buys the house from the Church, as it was no longer used as a monastery or occupied by monks, and then discovers the hidden trap shelf inside the tabernacle? I can't piece together how he found the keys, or how he located the trap shelf, but I'm sure the information was passed down from one generation to the other."

"Just one question," I asked: "why didn't they just sell the contents and live like kings?"

"Maybe they were too scared of revealing what they knew, and so ended up being the keeper of both the treasure and the conspiracy."

"Wow, how did Agostino manage to keep this to himself for all these years?"

I remembered his letter to me: *"Be careful; trust nobody."*

Chapter 13

Midweek, late at night, Figline was a very quiet place, making our break-in at the church so much easier.

Eddie slowly removed the slightly damaged pane of glass and put it safely against the wall, until it was time to place it back in its original place. We both squeezed ourselves through the narrow opening, and made our way toward the centre of the altar, facing the tabernacles on opposing walls. We started to walk slowly toward the tabernacle on the right, with only one thought going through our minds: *Please fit!*

With one turn of the key, we heard the lock click and we knew we were in. Eddie shone the torch into the space, as I searched for any movement of the inside panels, using the same method as before: anti-clockwise movements until the inside keyhole was exposed. I removed the chain around my neck, with both the keys Agostino left me, and put the larger of the two keys into the lock.

It seemed that, over the years, debris had fallen into the stonework, so I used a crowbar to remove enough of the stonework to expose the cavity wall. I plunged my hand inside the hollow gap within the cavity wall and pulled out a weighty pouch, which I found was tied to another pouch, then another, then another: four pouches and still one more tabernacle to open; it seemed that this was going to be the largest treasure trove so far to be uncovered!

With the adrenaline kicking in, we wasted no time in moving to the opposing side of the church and carrying out the same procedure, this time executing the job at hand like pros.

With both tabernacles emptied of jewels and a sealed package, possibly containing more letters or maps, it would have been easy to get careless, but we knew we had to cover our tracks, as this was in no way the end of the trail. After carefully making good the insides of the tabernacles, and cleaning any evidence to suggest foul play, we made our way to the vestry, to return the key that Eddie had "borrowed". But our good fortune seemed to have run out: the vestry door was locked! We had overlooked the possibility of not being able to gain entry. We had only one option: we decided to leave the key on the floor by the vestry door, where the priest or cleaner would find it, and hopefully think it had been accidentally dropped.

We then made our way to the narrow opening and climbed

out, passing the tools and the strings of pouches through the gap. I started to load the car, whilst Eddie replaced the pane of glass we had removed for our entry and escape back into position.

The first thing we did when we got back was empty the bags. The second was to stand back and stare dumbfounded at the amount of jewels we had found hidden in just that one place. The jewels found in San Biagio Church in Borro were no comparison to what we had just unveiled.

Olivia could hear us and joined us in the sitting room. The three of us were overwhelmed, and remained in silence for a while longer, just staring at the magnificent collection of gold, diamonds, rubies and emeralds encrusting a variety of pieces, from crosses to brooches to rings; it was a kaleidoscope of colour.

I broke the silence by asking Olivia how she was, without turning my gaze away from the jewels; Olivia answered "fine" in the same fashion. In a daze, she reached over and picked up the package, slowly removing its contents to reveal another map and a letter, no doubt written in Latin.

We were all feeling pretty shattered now, and decided to call it a night.

It seemed that most of the morning had already gone when we finally woke. I opened the shutters, to the sounds of the hustle and bustle of the square. Olivia made coffee in the largest percolator she could find, and poured us both a cup.

"I don't believe it," I said, in amusement; "Eddie is already dressed and strolling around the market."

Olivia joined me at the window and called down to him: "What's the matter? Couldn't you sleep?"

Eddie called up: "Good morning, beautiful people. I'm going to the shops, to buy some treats to bring over."

"Well, that's pretty decent of you, old chap," I replied.

With that, Eddie continued walking toward the confectionery stall. It seemed that others had the same idea as the stall was very popular, with hands reaching out to grab the array of goodies on offer. This proved to work in Eddie's favour, as he was about to discover.

Olivia picked up the letter – or "scroll", as it was called back in the day – and sat down with her second cup of coffee. I knew Olivia might be there for a while, so I decided to take time out and have a long soak in the bath, hopefully energized and ready for Eddie to come over, to put a rough value on our latest goods.

The bell rang and I pressed the buzzer so Eddie could come up. He looked very pleased with himself and greeted Olivia with a kiss on the hand, before handing over pieces of assorted nougat, displayed in a woven basket wrapped with cellophane and red ribbons.

"Hello, mate. What's put that beaming smile on your face? Wait a minute – you've either won the lottery or been chatting to a girl!"

Eddie seemed excited to share his joy. "First of all, she's not a girl, but definitely all woman!" He told us that there was a crowd around the confectionery stall, going on to say: "There were hands picking up items all over the place, and as I grabbed a basket of assorted nougat, I looked up and saw that I was holding the same basket as a beautiful brunette, with a smile which made my lips twitch. We each gestured for the other to take the basket, and all the while I was trying hard to think up a way I could get to see her again. It might seem corny, but the first thing that came into my head was: 'How about sharing the nougat, by joining me for a coffee?'"

I don't know how Olivia and I didn't burst into laughter, as Eddie continued: "Don't look at me like that; it worked! Gianna – that's her name – joined me for coffee and said, although it was the worst chat-up line she had heard, it made her laugh, and she appreciated my spontaneity. So, we have exchanged phone numbers and arranged to take a trip to Sienna together. Gianna knows Sienna very well, as she used to work there for a while."

I was happy for him, but pulled his leg a little. "You so and so! Her name suggests she's Italian, but by the sound of things she speaks excellent English."

Eddie replied: "Lucky for me, Gianna spent two years studying in England, so she speaks pretty good English. Who knows, if all goes well she might teach me Italian?"

Olivia piped up: "Looks like you forgot to share the nougat; this package hasn't been opened."

We all laughed and looked forward to meeting Gianna. I asked Eddie if this meant his mind was too preoccupied to value our new treasure, to which he just grinned and picked up paper, pen and magnifying glass, to begin the task at hand.

I went and sat next to Olivia on the couch. Judging by the writing on the pad which lay beside her, she had managed to translate quite a lot of the manuscript. Olivia looked up and began quoting the Latin:

"'Pater dilecte Fratine, quoniam ultima congressus est cum vos adepti sumus talibus auxiliis, et omnes in favorem bellum

aduersus Angliam. Quamquam Italiae provinciis auxilia ex pluribus nobilibus nobiles Francie, qui tempus suum largitor magis quam opibus egere tamen pecuniaque inveniamur. Sicut semper mi carissime scio Numerare possum super vos et congregatio San Dominici Ecclesia et thye negotiatores Arretium valde esse liberalem. Necessarius est ut consequemur necessaria pecunia aliter missio nostra erit deserta.'"

"Okay, Miss Clever-Clogs, can we now have the English version, please?"

She smiled and translated as follows: "Okay, are you sitting comfortably?

> *"'Dear Father Fratine, since my last meeting with you we have gained much support, and all in favour of declaring war on England. Although we have the support of the nobles from numerous provinces of Italy, and some of the nobles of France, who have been more than generous with their time and wealth, we still find ourselves in need of more funds. As always, my dear friend, I know I can count on you, the congregation of San Domenico Church and the merchants of Arezzo to be very generous. It is imperative that we achieve the necessary funds, otherwise our mission will be abandoned.*

Signed,

Cardinal Bertocelli.'"

Olivia's translation had given us the name of the next church to locate. I cross-referenced the church Cardinal Bertocelli mentioned, with the original map that we found at San Biagio, Borro, corroborating that our next stop was San Domenico.

The phone rang.

"Ciao, Nathan, it's Marco. I forgot to mention the last time you were here that it is Stefano's birthday this coming Friday. I wanted to invite my family and friends to celebrate, so please come and bring your friends, too."

It was a good opportunity to catch up with the family, as it seemed we were all too busy lately; I eagerly accepted.

As I hung up, I was shocked by Eddie cursing.

"Fuck! Excuse my French, guys, but there's enough here to feed a whole village for a year!"

Turning eagerly toward Eddie, I smirked proudly, and waited with anticipation to hear his valuation of our latest jewel find.

"At worst, this lot is worth no less than two-hundred k, but I think will fetch nearer three-hundred." We all remained seated in silence, stunned at what Eddie had just revealed.

Then, calmly, I opened a bottle of red wine and poured it into three large wine glasses, to toast our fortune.

We had built our own secret wall in the attic, and placed the jewels inside for safekeeping, until we could arrange another meeting with our friends in Antwerp. The only problem we faced was that the price tag for the new bundle was at least three or maybe four times the previous price. This was now getting serious, and I started to feel a little concerned.

*

Friday soon came around, and Eddie went to meet Gianna in the town centre. He had called to ask if she wanted to accompany him to a child's birthday party, explaining that it was his friend's second-cousin's birthday, and he would love her to be his plus-one. She found the phrase amusing, and Eddie had to clarify that it meant he wanted her to be his guest. So, when the doorbell rang, it was Eddie and who I guessed was Gianna. We called to them from the window that we were on our way down, and Eddie introduced his new love to me and Olivia. It was pretty obvious from his body language that he was smitten.

When we arrived at Marco and Antonella's house, I felt a warm feeling inside: happiness radiating from being around both the young and old; there were at least fifteen children under the age of thirteen playing in the garden. Roberto was in high spirits, enjoying a laugh and jovial banter with a few of our cousins and other family members, catching up with each other's news. This was the part of my Italian heritage that I missed back in Brighton, and I was happy to be a part of it again.

Marco bellowed that the food was ready, and signalled with his hand for everyone to come and enjoy. Young and old made their way into the large dining room. The adults sat around two rectangular dining tables, pushed together and covered in a patterned plastic cover; the children had a separate table, decorated with dragon-themed cups and plates, because dragons were the birthday boy's favourite thing. Auntie Marie blessed the food we were about to dive into, and Marco asked us all to raise our glasses, to toast his son's twelfth birthday.

I noticed that he kept looking at Eddie's girlfriend and wished he would stop; it was making me feel uncomfortable. And, if I could see what he was doing, it only followed that others – specifically Eddie and Antonella – would notice, too.

Later that evening, Marco asked Olivia if it was okay for him to snatch me away, for a stroll in the garden. Olivia was pleased to be asked, herself busy getting better acquainted with the other ladies.

"How long has your friend known Gianna?"

I thought this was an unusual question to ask, but I went along with it, and told him it was a few days ago.

"She's a policewoman. I just thought you should know."

I thanked Marco for the warning. At least he had now replaced one concern with another; on the one hand I was happy to know that my cousin was not making advances toward Eddie's girl, and on the other I now had to tell Eddie his new love was an officer of the law.

We went back inside, just in time for Antonella to dim the lights, so that we could sing happy birthday to Stefano. Everyone shouted for him to make a wish – and to remember that he was only twelve! We laughed.

We stayed a while longer, before making our way home. I was the designated driver that evening, so I was as sober as a judge. I dropped Eddie and Gianna in the town centre, after making polite chat about hoping to see her soon; *blah, blah, blah.* As soon as we got home, I confided in Olivia about the conversation I'd had with Marco regarding Gianna.

I could see that Olivia was saddened, as she knew this might mean Eddie would have to stop seeing her. "That would be so sad. It's obvious that he thinks she's someone special, and I get the feeling that she likes him, too."

I looked at Olivia and nodded; "Eddie isn't stupid: he won't jeopardize our mission for a woman."

The room went quiet, and I immediately cursed my error.

I got the verbal attack with both barrels: "So, the mission is more important than a woman, huh?! Now I know what you think of women, I will act accordingly!"

"For God's sake. He's only just met her, is what I meant. Stop looking for reasons to have a dig at me. I thought all those uncertainties between us were put to bed. I just can't see how it will pan out if Eddie continues this relationship; he would be asking her to choose between her ethics as a copper and her loyalty to him. Knowing who she is so early on is a bonus; it gives Eddie the opportunity to end it, before someone gets hurt."

Surprisingly, Eddie called me later that night, to say that he had walked Gianna home before going back to the flat.

"I really like her, Nathan," he added, out of the blue.

"Great you've gone all soppy on me."

I decided to break the news to him in the morning, and let him go to bed feeling content. "Goodnight, mate. See you tomorrow."

Chapter 14

Eddie came around bright and early the next day, ready for our trip to central Arezzo.

I felt there was a small matter to take care of first – okay, maybe not that small and perhaps a little awkward to boot, but it had to be done. I asked Eddie to come and take a walk with me. I was not looking forward to telling my friend the news. I decided not to beat around the bush, and told Eddie word for word what Marco had told me.

I watched as Eddie's face dropped. I knew this was going to be a difficult decision for him, so I made it easy, telling him that I would totally understand if he wanted to take his share of the spoils to date and go and live happily ever after with his Gianna, with no hard feelings.

"Let's leave things as they are," he answered. "What started out to be an escape from reality – and, of course, monetary gain – has become something far more rewarding. I came over to help you discover treasure and became involved in something far bigger. This has been one of the best times of my life, Nathan, and I have felt alive. I am proud of what we are slowly unravelling, and I want to continue on our mission. I will do my best to shield Gianna, by making no reference to it, and perhaps, for both our sakes, will take things a little slower."

"Eddie, this may mean you will be living a double life for a while. Can you do that?"

"I'm not happy with the situation, but I'm not prepared to close the door on either; I want to see what we have started through to the end and, truth be told, I also want to continue my relationship with Gianna. Come on, Nathan, why can't I have both?"

I felt a little uncomfortable with the situation, but just added: "Fair enough."

We left the matter at that, and went back to pick up Olivia, for our journey to central Arezzo.

San Domenico was easy to spot. Although humble in decor, it stood proud in the piazza, with its two bells and yellow stone structure. Its exterior gave an impression of modesty, as there were no ornate figurines or archangels adorning the facets of the building, and once you stepped inside, the same could be said again.

As with the majority of Dominicans, San Domenico was supported by an alms charity which was set up to fund the poor. If this was the case, then not only were the nobles conspiring to plot against the Vatican, but also to take from a charity set up to support the most needy.

Although the inside was drab and eerily dark, at closer inspection the church did house an abundance of paintings, including a monumental crucifix as ornate as any I have seen. There were still traces of the frescos which once ordained this desolate but still peaceful church. The church was called Basilica Di San Domenico, otherwise known as "the nave with the wooden roof". Perhaps the carpenter in me appreciated the work involved in creating such a structured piece, because for some strange reason I felt a connection here, an attachment I hadn't felt with any other place of worship.

I noticed the tabernacle which, unlike the previous churches, faced the congregation. What also stood out for me was the contrast of the exquisite wooden carvings decorating the tabernacle to the subtleness of the decor of the rest of the church. It was by far the most elaborately carved of all that we had seen – almost as if the architect wanted to draw our eyes to it. The tabernacle was flanked by an ornate stone frame, and carved and painted on the actual door was a cross with eight points, painted in red, and a bishop's hat in black and gold. This seemed strange, because it made the tabernacle look out of place. What was significant about the red cross? Was the cardinal an ancestor of the Knights Templar of King George?

We all headed outside and left Olivia to digest the literature she had picked up. As the lighting was pretty poor inside the church, Olivia sat herself on a bench in the grounds, whilst Eddie and I went to investigate the perimeters of the church, to see what weak spots we could find, should we need to break in.

We couldn't believe our good fortune, when we walked to the back of the church to find a large courtyard, with iron gates left wide open. It seemed that the courtyard was being used as a car park and, although there was enough ground to accommodate car parking sufficient for an average size wedding, the area was unkempt, with its fair share of potholes and uneven surfaces. This was going to be a piece of cake – if you'll excuse the pun. The back entrance was hidden from view by a low wall, and accessed via walking down a few steps. I looked at Eddie and, without saying a word, rubbed my hands together and gave him a thumbs-up; this was going to be easy.

We were still sitting on the wall when the door in question opened, and a group of people with nametags on lanyards around their necks walked past us obliviously, chatting amongst themselves. As soon as they were out of sight, we made our way down toward the steps and opened the door, which led us inside the building.

In front of us was a narrow corridor, with two doors on the right-hand side and two on the left. We turned the handle on each door. The first two rooms were empty, and must have been used by the people who passed us outside. We were not so fortunate with the third door, and found ourselves face to face with two young ladies who gave us an inquisitive look. Making our excuses, we closed the door and hurriedly headed toward the last of the four doors. Hallelujah; this led us straight into the church! What a result!

Walking back out, we saw Olivia chatting to some locals. I stood back and admired her for a while, before walking over and wrapping an arm around her waist.

Following our recce, we were all a little hungry, and found a typically quaint Mediterranean restaurant, for a bite to eat. We ordered the establishment's famous steak Florentine, for the three of us to share, with two portions of homemade chips, a small bowl of fasulye served with baby spinach, drizzled with olive oil, lemon and basil, and a medium-sized bowl of salad. With a little persuasion from the waiter, we agreed to add a bowl of fresh, uncut artisan bread and a carafe of red wine. We'd all tasted steak Florentine before, but agreed that this was our favourite; I wanted to savour every mouthful. Olivia described the experience to unwrapping a masterpiece with your tastebuds. We then drank a toast to our health and enjoyed the feast prepared for us.

"You seemed engrossed in your conversation earlier. What were you talking with the locals about, sweetheart?" I enquired.

"I was fascinated with the place. I saw a sign for Piazza Grande, and was asking the locals how far away it was. They informed me that it was one of the most beautiful squares in the whole of Italy, and only about ten minutes away. In particular they recommended a visit to Palazzo Della Loggia, with its many shops. They seemed optimistic that I would enjoy my visit, and if I was passing this way again, to drop in and let them know what I thought of the area. They explained that they were here most days between ten a.m. and one p.m., undertaking many duties as volunteers in the church."

"Well, there's no time like the present. Shall we pay a visit to

Piazza Grande?" I suggested.

With all in agreement, we paid the bill and made our way to the famous piazza. Eddie and I found a small cafeteria, to sit and enjoy an espresso, while Olivia fleeted in and out of the shops. In full flow with our plans to gain access to the tabernacle at San Domenico, I had an idea and hoped Olivia would be up for it.

Olivia was soon heading back toward us, so I signalled with a shake of a hand if she wanted a drink. She put her bags of shopping on an empty chair, picked up the drinks menu and settled for an Aperol spritz. I waited for Olivia to take a sip of her drink, before broaching my idea.

"Well, I think now you've visited this great place that it would be a good idea for you to go back and tell your volunteer friends at San Domenico what you thought of the Piazza Grande."

Olivia seemed to like the idea and replied: "Aah, that's so thoughtful of you. I'd like that."

Treading carefully, I went on to ask: "How about joining your new friends for a day or so? You could say that you have a few spare hours this week, and wondered if there could be some way to help out – you know, to show your appreciation."

Olivia looked at me suspiciously. "Okay, what are you up to, Nathan Doyle?"

I explained that the back door led us straight into the church and, although the back door was open and provided us with access, this would only have been because there were still volunteers in the building. I also thought that the last volunteer would surely lock all four doors, meaning that the door leading to the church would also be locked.

"So, what are you expecting me to accomplish by volunteering there?" Olivia asked.

"We need a print of both keys: the key for the back door and the key to the inside of the church."

"Didn't we previously do our best to avoid that idea?"

"Yep, and it was great that we managed to gain access without going down this route; it means that we can use this method just this once. Marco won't know what the keys are for; at worst, he may be curious, that's all. So, I think we will be alright."

Thank goodness the Italians were more trusting than Olivia; she was welcome to start giving her services as soon as she wanted.

We commented that it might take Olivia two or three days to actually manage getting the plastic prints of the keys, and were surprised when she managed the task on her first shift.

Straight after, I dropped Olivia home, picked Eddie up and headed over to Marco's showroom.

He was sitting in his office when we arrived, and was pleased to see us. He offered us an espresso coffee, asking if we were just passing or jokingly wondering if we needed more "protection". I handed him the imprints.

"When do you need them made?"

I didn't want him to become too suspicious, so I casually said, "No hurry; the next couple of days will be fine," trying to disguise any urgency in the matter.

"Okay, I have a very good friend of mine who will do them for me, with no questions asked. I will call you when they are ready."

We stayed and made small-talk for a while, before bidding each other goodnight.

In no time, Olivia's stint as a volunteer was over. Olivia seemed to enjoy the three days helping at San Domenico and, today being her last volunteering shift, she asked me to pick her up an hour later than the previous two afternoons, as her friends wanted to take her for coffee before she left.

We drove home in silence and we ate in silence. After the meal, I raised my glass and toasted Olivia, saying: "Who knows? One day you may meet up with your friends again."

Olivia gathered enough information in those three days to know that the church was unoccupied between one p.m. and five p.m., with the priest always the first to return. Apparently, he always reopened the doors at five p.m., then spent twenty minutes in prayer before preparing for the six p.m. evening service.

Marco had called to say that our keys were ready, so we arranged to pick them up before heading to San Domenico. That evening, we were going to try out a dummy run. We needed to know roughly how long it would take us to drive to and park in the courtyard, get into the church, presumably remove the cavity wall inside the tabernacle and, if our hunch was correct, extract the treasure. Of course, this plan would only work if Agostino's keys fitted the tabernacle – else it would be back to the drawing board. We estimated that four hours would be ample time, providing that the damage to the interior was not excessive. There seemed to be a few areas in which we would need luck on our side, but it was a risk we were prepared to take.

The next day, the car was loaded with the necessary tools. By midday we were in Central Arezzo.

We chose a busy café to take refreshments and prepare for the task ahead. Then I kissed Olivia goodbye, and made my way with Eddie on foot to the church. Olivia was going to drive back home and return to Arezzo around three p.m.; we agreed that I would call her on her mobile and let it ring three times, to signal that we were ready to be picked up.

The first key fitted, and we made our way along the corridor toward the fourth door, which opened straight into the church. The second key fitted and we were inside. Marco had done us proud.

I pulled out my own tabernacle keys, ready to try the lock, but as we approached the wooden door we noticed that it was already open. There was a copy of the Bible placed on a silver tray, which I removed and placed to one side, within sight, to remind me to replace it when we had finished.

As previously, I tried turning the back panel anti-clockwise, to see if this would reveal the same keyhole as previously, but it did not work. I tapped the sides of the walls, and pointed out to Eddie that the back wall was hollow.

From his kit, Eddie brought out a bolster hammer and a small crowbar; laying a dust sheet to catch any debris, he began chipping the stone which was slotted over the back panel. Eddie took his time, ensuring that minimal repairs would be needed. He made the necessary opening, and stood back to allow me access. Eddie supported my weight, as I pushed myself as far down the hollow opening as possible.

I didn't have to stretch too far before my hand felt a smooth object. Slowly, I managed to retrieve a rectangular box. This time there were no pouches; just the box.

Working together, we carefully restored the tabernacle to how we found it, placing the Bible on the silver tray back where it had been, and made our call to Olivia.

As we drove back to Terranuova, the accelerating adrenalin filled the car.

Back home, I placed the rectangular box on the sitting room table and, with three pairs of eyes glued to the box, I slowly opened the lid.

It seemed that we had captured a night of a thousand stars in a box! Cut diamonds sparkled in their droves. There were hundreds, maybe thousands of them, in a multitude of different dimensions. The value of this collection was surely going to be huge.

There was a piece of discoloured paper sticking out from the box's lining; on closer inspection, I could see that there was an additional compartment. Using a flat knife, I carefully lifted the section to reveal further letters. I passed the letters to Olivia.

She looked cheekily at the diamonds, then at the letters, and said: "Thank you, darling, but I would prefer the other contents."

Chapter 15

The gems were left in the tin we found them in, and stored safely within the false wall Eddie and I had built in the cantina. For extra precaution, the only route into the hollow wall was via the utility area, disguised by wooden panelling, with the washing machine blocking its entrance. Eddie had already established that the quality of the stones found at San Domenico was second to none, and would demand a substantial retail tag – perhaps even more than our previous gains.

We decided to lie low for a few months.

During the day, I helped Eddie with odd jobs which needed doing to his flat, and in the evenings I enjoyed time with Olivia and family members. Olivia took time out to go back to London, to ensure that her flat was okay and catch up with friends.

It was when driving her to the airport, for one of these visits, that I made a suggestion to her: "How do you feel about renting out your flat and staying here permanently?"

She answered coolly: "I suppose it makes sense. I'll give it some thought whilst I'm over there."

Not wanting to rush her, I accepted her answer and turned up the radio.

Eddie saw Gianna on average twice a week. The rest of the time he would come over to mine. I sometimes wondered if it was to see me, or to be closer to his treasure haul.

Olivia was due back tomorrow, so I decided to spruce up the house and get an early night. I took one of the maps to bed with me, for some light bedtime reading.

Looking at the marked spots on the map, I could see there were still six towns with a church potentially used by the conspirators; I wrote down the names of each: Bucine, Castelfranco, Loro Ciuffenna, Pian di Scò and Moncioni, and, of course, Montevarchi. All six were so close in proximity that one could easily visit them in a day, but we were not taking in the sights; each place needed to be given its own allocated time.

The next day, I picked Olivia up from the airport and took her straight home. I wanted tonight to be totally about her. The dinner table was set, and her bathrobe and fragrant bath salts were prepared, for Olivia to take a soak. Her favourite C.D. was playing in the background.

"This is nice," she smiled. "What's the special occasion?"

I looked at her a little surprised, and replied: "No occasion. I just wanted to let you know how much you mean to me."

She kissed me and softly whispered: "You can show me how much I mean to you after dinner."

The next evening, Eddie came over and continued compiling the estimated values of the latest items.

After a few hours, Eddie muttered: "I think someone had better pour three large cups of strong espresso – and maybe add a drop of Grappa, to calm the nerves."

Eddie waited until we all had a drink in hand, before adding, in a matter-of-fact manner: "This little metal box contains a fortune to a king! The minimum value of these uncut diamonds is… well, I would say the absolute lowest..."

"Eddie, put us out of our misery, mate! Just tell us how much," I asked in anticipation.

Eddie took a gulp of his spiked coffee and calmly said: "The value of the diamonds is a cool two-and-a-half-million pounds... at least."

Even after expenses, I knew that we already had an estimated three-hundred-and-sixty-thousand pounds hidden downstairs, in the cantina – and, my god, this was not including our latest and biggest find. Not to mention the potential for what the remaining marked churches could provide. My mind was swirling with a mixture of fear and excitement. The stars were within our grasp; we were on our way to becoming multi-millionaires!

I shook my head, thinking: *No, no, Nathan, this is wrong! This is not our money; somehow we will have to give it back to the Italian authorities… to the people.*

The valuation should have made all of us very happy, but I was starting to feel uneasy, and concerned about what consequences may be presented. We hadn't just taken this treasure, but we were also unravelling the secrets of the manuscripts and letters, which could change what we know about history. I wished Agostino was around, to advise me. I wished I wasn't frightened for all of our safety, especially Olivia's. I consoled myself with the fact that these treasures were buried, even lost or forgotten, over the centuries.

I looked over at Olivia, hoping that the collection of Latin messages she was studiously translating for us was going to throw some light on that which was plotted hundreds of years ago.

"I'm sorry, boys, since my return from London I haven't had time to completely translate the latest letter that you found at San Domenico. Unfortunately, without any assistance other than the internet, I can only part-translate this one – and it doesn't really make sense to me. So far, what I am reading says:

"*'Dear Father Servi ... Arezzo ... We have twenty-one nobles in Arezzo ... with Ferrara, Sienna and Naples. We ... have a ... one-hundred and sixty ships, twenty ... and a ... We have ... ships and ... thirty ... and fifty thousand men ... four thousand ... With the ... French ... we will ... England and its King! I .... and ... ships ... 1538. ... March ... the King ... I will ... to keep the back ... open from 9.00 p.m. to 10.00 p.m. ... the last Monday of each month ... our mission is completed...'*

"Something... I can't make out the next sentence, apart from the words *'twelve churches'*, *'Bishop Sabattani'*, *'Terranuova'* and that it is signed by Cardinal Bertocelli."

Olivia said that she would take the letter to the library in the morning, as she could go no further with her translation. She put the relevant documents in her black portfolio bag and put it to one side until tomorrow.

"I'll come with you," I offered.

She replied: "Only to drop me off, darling; I can't concentrate when you're around."

I was quick to reply: "Is that because I'm irresistible?"

"No, Nathan, because you will keep interrupting me."

We laughed.

Whilst continuing to make small-talk, my thoughts were trying to digest that which Olivia had managed to translate. I wondered what the number twelve in the Cardinal's letter could refer to.

So far, we had three maps to view, one found at each church already visited. I placed them on the wooden table, in the order we found them. All three maps showed hundreds of churches, however, I noticed on the first that there was only one church with an added drawing of a crucifix above its steeple. I looked at the second map, and now noticed that there were two churches marked in the same way. As I glanced quickly at the third map staring back at me, it became clear that the maps were explaining to the person in receipt of them which church was the next used to conceal the funds raised, and where the next clue to what they were conspiring in would be. On further inspection, I noticed that, on all three maps, there were also some churches underlined in faint silver foil, including the three marked with a crucifix above the steeple.

Oh, my god! It was staring me in the face! I counted the

churches underlined with the silver foil, and ascertained that there were twelve. Cardinal Bertocelli was writing to the twelve churches where donations were taken.

We had already identified three churches, meaning there were another nine to visit. This also led me to believe that the crucifixes were added to the churches on each map when the treasure was deposited inside the tabernacle, and before the next map added to the hoard.

Olivia's trip to the library the next day paid off, as by the following evening she had managed to translate the remaining parts of the letter.

"Dear Father Servio,

The citizens of Arezzo have given generously. We have twenty-one nobles in Arezzo, ready to join forces with Ferrara, Sienna and Naples. We already have a fleet of one-hundred and sixty ships, twenty heavy cannons and a number of siege machines. In addition, we have accrued large ships and supplies, thirty galleys, fifty thousand men at arms and four thousand horses. With the help of our

French comrades, we will destroy England and its King! I urge us to remain diligent and continue to raise funds, to acquire more ships and cannons. Every detail must be in place very soon, as we aim to carry out our mission in the springtime of 1538. The month of March is favoured to attack, as this is when the King is preoccupied with arranging sporting activities.

As always, please remember to keep our correspondence and meetings to a minimum. However, I will continue to keep the back door open from 9.00 p.m. to 10.00 p.m. on the last Monday of each month, for any urgent meetings, until our mission is completed.

With only two seasons left of this year, I have handed over the responsibility of running the twelve churches under my diocese to the Bishop Sabattani, and I will remain here in Terranuova until our mission is completed.

Signed

Cardinal Bertocelli."

Where on Earth would someone hide such an armada of ships without this becoming common knowledge to outsiders – and, of course, without someone in the Vatican hearing about their intentions? Perhaps France was playing a bigger part, and was keeping some or all the fleet in one of their harbours?

I knew that Cardinal Bertocelli was based in Terranuova at the time; I would assume that living locally to the main church in the piazza would benefit the cause. If I was the cardinal, I would want to reside somewhere I could easily keep a watchful eye, especially on the last Monday of each month, when I (he) would have to keep the church unlocked for any messaging services, etc. It was becoming more and more apparent that my house was a very strong candidate for the cardinal's accommodation; I wondered if he could have been a previous tenant. If this was so, people would not believe the history attached to my humble abode. If my hunch was correct, the value of this property would treble!

The next few weeks were spent taking visits to wherever the churches marked on the map took us.

By day, Eddie continued to assess the value of the takings, and by night he enjoyed meeting up with Gianna. I could tell Eddie was smitten, and it wouldn't be long before he wanted to take the relationship further. I just hoped he could keep his private life and our mission separate, until our assignment was completed.

We continued to use the tried and tested procedure, as before, always making sure that we cleaned up after ourselves, so nobody would know that we had been there at all. The stashes were becoming less exhilarating than before, but we were determined to complete the puzzle.

Olivia was quieter than normal, and I had put it down to what we were discovering. But it now seemed that it was due to a more personal matter. Then, one day she sat down and informed me: “Nathan I have a little matter which needs discussing.”

I looked at her intensely and she continued: “The tenancy on my flat is coming up for renewal, and I was wondering what I should do.”

Joking, I asked her if she had any intentions of going back to live there. Without hesitation, Olivia replied: “Well, I’m not going to give up my independence with no concrete future to look forward to!”

“Our future is together,” I assured her. “That in turn means that whatever I have is yours, too. So, shall we make a joint decision now, and let the flat go?”

Olivia agreed with a nod, and we sealed the decision with a romantic siesta.

I knew Olivia wanted more. However, for now I wanted to remain focused on completing what we had started – not just for me but for Nono Agostino.

There was going to be plenty to sort out back in England: furniture to either sell or have shipped over, cutting ties with whatever we needed to and committing ourselves to our new lives in Italy. So, on this occasion it was Eddie dropping me and Olivia at Pisa airport, for our trip back to England.

Once there, we cleared Olivia's flat, taking any wanted items to my property in Brighton, and donated unwanted items to friends and the local charity shops. In a strange way, it was good to be back.

The tenants had kept my house and garden in very good order, for which I was very grateful, and although we certainly did not need the money anymore, Olivia and I agreed it would be best to keep a home in England for occasional visits. As the tenants had proven to be reliable and respectful to my property, I decided to extend their tenancy agreement for a year. This gave me the peace of mind that the home was not left empty and, as already shown, would be taken care of.

When business was taken care of, we then made the most of our trip, visiting old friends and colleagues.

Although I remained in constant communication with my pal Danny, I left out the fact that I was coming over, as I wanted to surprise him. We arrived at the yard just before lunchtime, and as soon as some of the guys spotted us, they came over to greet us. I thought they were more interested in meeting Olivia; *Typical builders*. But, it reminded me that this place was not just a business to me, but a home, full of people I felt connected to.

Danny must have heard the laughter and commotion, and he came out of the office to see what was occurring. His eyes lit up and he walked over to give me a heartfelt hug. We slowly walked into the office to catch up. I complimented him on shedding a few pounds, and we laughed when he informed me that he had joined Weight Watchers. I pulled his leg that I bet it was to meet the opposite sex.

“Better than dating sites,” he laughed.

We pulled each other’s leg for a while longer, before coming back to the business. Danny had run the place well; I knew how much the business and the staff meant to him. I’d decided I wanted to give him the opportunity to become sole owner of the business. But I knew Danny was a very proud man, and it would offend him if I were to hand over the business for nothing. Besides, business is business. So, instead I made him an offer I knew he wouldn't be able to refuse.

"Danny, I have decided to lay roots in Italy, and only come back to England for vacations. So, if you are interested, I want to give you first refusal on my share of the business. What do you think?"

"Wow, this is unexpected, Nathan. I mean, I have enjoyed running the business with you and by myself, so I'm happy either way, mate. It depends if I can afford to buy your share. How much are you thinking of selling for?"

"I'll be honest, mate, I'm doing pretty well with projects I've become involved with in Italy. Because of this, and because I really don't need the hassle of negotiating with potential buyers – and because, mate, it's me and you who have built the business to what it is today – I thought you could take my share off my hands for sixty thousand. Would you be interested?"

I could see I was fooling nobody with such a low offer, and Danny's reply confirmed this: "Nathan, I know as well as you do that the business, stock and vans are worth over two-hundred. I'm making a good living, with you just taking a small percentage as a silent partner, but I can't let you gift me forty k!"

Danny then wanted to know more about what I was involved with in Italy. Without telling him about the treasure, I tried to explain that I had landed on my feet, and had several projects, which my cousin had thrown my way to occupy me. I went on to explain that in many ways he would be doing me a favour by taking the business off my hands.

"Well, put like that, how can I refuse? Yes, of course I accept your proposal." We hugged and Danny added: "Thanks, mate. I just want you to know that, if things don't work out for you over there, I'll always sell you back your share, with the same generosity as you've shown me."

"Let's get out of here now, before you see me cry!"

We completed the necessary paperwork, and Danny insisted he take me and Olivia and for dinner, to celebrate.

It was a great evening, reminiscing and sharing some of our antics with Olivia. Danny was the salt of the earth, and I was fortunate to be his friend. I hoped he would take up the invitation to come over and stay with us someday – who knew, perhaps even meet that special someone?

We said our goodbyes and took a taxi to the boutique B-and-B we had booked for the night, a little worse for wear after consuming more alcohol than food.

Olivia was getting ready for bed and, as I lay on the bed, I caught a glimmer of her slender silhouette through the open door of the en-suite bathroom; I watched as she moisturized her whole body, before slipping a tantalizing camisole over her naked skin. She looked stunning, so naturally beautiful, and she was mine!

Olivia stood at the edge of the bed and asked curiously: "You okay?"

Pulling her toward me, I whispered: "Never been better."

The next day, we had planned to spend the day in London, when I received a phone call from Danny, apologizing for any inconvenience and asking me to drop into the yard, as there were a few things he wanted to go over with me, before I headed back to Italy.

"Eh, okay, mate. What time is good for you?"

"Shall we say one o'clock?"

"Yep, see you at one."

Olivia looked over at me and smiled. "Go see Danny, and I'll take the opportunity to surprise my former colleagues. I know just where they will be at one o'clock: their and my favourite haunt."

We made arrangements for me to meet Olivia later that afternoon; this would give Olivia the chance to catch up with her old colleagues – and, no doubt, discuss me to some extent.

Olivia wore a pale-blue cotton shirt tucked into a pair of fitted, black designer jeans. It reminded me of the day I walked back into her life again. I wondered if Olivia also realized that she had chosen the same outfit to wear as she had worn on that day – the day our relationship entered a new chapter.

"You look stunning; I've never felt prouder than I do at this moment. Thank you for giving me a second chance."

Olivia gave me a blushing pout, followed by a gentle kiss, and in that moment everything external did not exist. I breathed in the moment, holding my girl tenderly in my arms, wanting to freeze time forever.

Before heading over to meet with Danny, I dropped Olivia off at Brighton station and watched her as she disappeared out of sight.

As I walked into the yard, I could see a large banner shouting the words: *"THIS IS NOT GOODBYE, BUT AU-REVOIR! GOOD LUCK, NATHAN. KEEP IN TOUCH."* No one was in the yard, and I stood in silence for a moment, staring at the banner. I could feel my eyes beginning to well up.

The moment was suddenly hijacked by my former staff – my friends – singing: *"For he's a jolly good fellow."* They were walking toward me, plastic cups filled with Champagne, one of which was thrust into my hand. In unison, they then started to chant: "Speech! Speech! Speech!"

I could barely speak from the emotion I was feeling, and I opened my mouth wide so that I would be heard. "I have enjoyed every year here, working with the best craftsmen in the country —"

At that, someone called out: "What do you mean, in the country? In the world!"

We all laughed and I continued: "I stand corrected; in the *world.* There have been times when we were not doing so well, yet none of you left to find better prospects; you remained loyal to Danny and I – that, my friends, is priceless. And I will always class each and every one of you my friends. I know I speak for Danny, too, when I say that a company is only as good as the team it employs, and you're a team which works together to keep the standards high, which in turn secures repeated business and continues to advance our reputation. It has been an honour to work with you and I hope I will always be welcome to come and visit you. Thank you, guys, from the bottom of my heart."

I was glad when the guys started cheering. I finished by saluting them, and followed Danny into the office.

"So, these were the business matters you needed me for?"

Danny smirked. "You didn't expect me to let you go without the team sending you off, did you?"

So, with that "business" out of the way, I asked Danny if he had any plans for the place.

"I'm not a greedy man, Nathan. Business is ticking over nicely, without me having to break my neck to make a decent living. The cherry on the icing is now being able to say it's mine. It feels good, Nathan. I know you could have got more for the place so, again, thanks; I do appreciate it."

We got a little soppy again and, after exchanging pleasantries and reiterating the desire to stay in touch, I bade my friend farewell. There were now only a couple of men on site, as I exited through the yard, and I nodded to them. I walked out feeling that the business was left in the right hands.

I got off at Kensington and made my way to Nick the Greek's

Taverna. I went straight inside, sat at the bar and ordered a Mythos beer.

I could see Olivia's reflection in the mirror, which was hanging on the wall in front of the bar. I slowly turned to face her and stared at my beautiful woman, watching her eyes gleaming as she talked animatedly, making gestures with her hands; she looked so happy telling her tales.

Then she spotted me. She gave me a photogenic stare, before getting up and walking toward me. "Hello, handsome, fancy seeing you here. Do you fancy buying a damsel a drink?"

"What would you like? No, let me guess: would the lady be interested in a Mojito with plenty of ice?"

"I think the lady definitely would."

We took our drinks over to Olivia's former colleagues, Olivia in front and me following, with a hand on her shoulder, as if needing a guide. I enjoyed being introduced to the people in the group who had not met me before, and to those who had seen and heard of but never spoken to me. One buxom lady, introduced to me as Rose, greeted me: "So, you're Nathan?" The look in her eyes said, in capital letters: "DON'T YOU DARE HURT HER AGAIN!"

I looked back at her without saying a word, hoping that she

could sense my attempt at reassurance that I had no intentions of doing so. I got the impression that Rose was far from as delicate as her name would suggest, and would get on anyone's case if they upset people she cared about.

The rest of the evening was pleasant, with stories of things that had happened over the years, some humorous, others of solidarity to each other in times of need.

It was soon time to say our goodbyes, with the promise of staying in touch. I wondered if Olivia was sad to be leaving this chapter firmly in the past.

We got back to Brighton station just before eleven o'clock.

"Shall we walk, or do you want to get a taxi?"

"You must have read my mind, Nathan. A slow stroll would be nice."

"Are you okay?"

"If you mean do I have any regrets, then the answer is categorically no; I wouldn't have swapped the last year for anything in this world... well, apart from front seats on the first passenger flight to Mars."

I brought her hand up to my mouth and kissed it tenderly, knowing that my love for her was reciprocated. Who could ask for more?

After three weeks of packing, handing back the keys to the flat, sifting through numerous letters, selling my half of the business and putting our bits and pieces in order, we were ready to go back to Italy.

"I wonder what Eddie's been up to while we've been gone?" I asked.

Olivia smiled and replied: "Most probably spending his third of the money spoiling Gianna."

The next morning, Danny turned up earlier than arranged, after insisting on driving all the way over from Lewes, to take us to the airport. Danny loaded the car with our luggage, as I settled the tab with the B-and-B.

I asked Danny to drive past my house in Brighton. I knew it was the right thing to do, keeping this place as a nest egg for me and Olivia – after all, we both had lifelong connections to England, of which we were both proud and would never want to surrender. I didn't feel that this was goodbye, but rather a feeling of being privileged by having homes in the two countries which meant so much to me. My father had served his country in the war, and my mother had brought many of her customs from Italy with her when she married my father – I felt they would be happy knowing that I had dual citizenship.

Gatwick airport was already heaving with arrivals and departures, but we had arrived in ample time. So, after checking in and bidding Danny ciao, we hit the duty-free shops, leaving ourselves nearly an hour to dine in style before boarding.

"Salute, darling. Let's drink a toast to our next chapter."

I raised my glass and added: "I'll drink to that, my beautiful darling."

As we came through arrivals, Eddie was already standing in the foyer, holding a placard with our names written in black, felt-tip pen: *"Nathan + Olivia"*. We could see he was pleased to see us. "Hi, guys, welcome back. It's good to see you both."

We caught up with each other's news all the way back to Terranuova. Eddie had a copy of my key, and we had agreed that he could stay at my place whilst we were away, to guard the expensive stash hidden in the cantina. Surprisingly, the flat was clean when we arrived. Olivia jokingly asked Eddie if Gianna had been coming around to do the chores.

Eddie looked hurt. "No, guys, I kept my promise to keep

Gianna out of our business. And, not wanting to jeopardize our relationship with lies, I decided not to spend too much time with her at the house. Anyway, what are you trying to say? I'm a changed man; I'm even wearing expensive aftershave!"

The evening was spent listening to Eddie updating us with the local news – and, of course, reiterating at least half a dozen times how wonderful his beautiful Gianna is. We finished a bottle of vino rosso and enjoyed a stress-free evening, which soon turned into another late night.

Olivia was the first to yawn, and Eddie took that as his cue to go back to his flat. He picked up his holdall and we watched him from the window, walking across the piazza to his abode.

Chapter 16

The next church on the list was Chiesa di Sant'Andrea a Cennano, in Montevarchi. The church was built in 1327 by Franciscans and, with the help of the Ricasoli family, it was restored several times. It had a complete restoration in 1772, which was designed by Giuseppe Cicori. My inner scholar felt blessed to be given this opportunity, to explore the history and architecture of these beautiful buildings, which I have always found interesting but lacked time to pursue.

Once inside the church, we proceeded to look for the familiar tabernacle, as in the previous churches, but to no avail. This completely threw us. What now?

We decided to take a break and put our thinking caps on over a cup of coffee.

"There has to be a tabernacle," I said, rubbing my forehead.

Olivia replied: "Who's to say there isn't? Remember, the church was renovated in 1772, and by the looks of some of the décor, I would not be surprised if further restorations were made at a later date; a tabernacle could now be concealed within the church walls by accident, rather than by any choices renovators might have made."

As we were discussing the possibilities of where the tabernacle may be hidden, my eyes were drawn upward, to a priest walking by in front of us, heading in the direction of the church.

Without any hesitation, I stood up and starting walking toward him. "There's only one way to find out."

"Nathan, come back," Eddie protested. "What is your plan? You can't just ask the question!"

I sat back down.

Between us, we hatched a plan that I would pretend to be a journalist, asking priests from churches of interest for an informal interview, as I was doing a documentary on the architect of Catholic churches – in particular, how sympathetically or not they had been restored. We were both satisfied with this angle of approach, so I headed off to find the priest.

With pen and pad in hand, courteously supplied by my beautiful assistant, I walked into the church and found the priest praying at the altar. I walked to the front of the church and stood in his view, waiting until he looked in my direction.

Within a few minutes, he introduced himself as Father Gioele, and I introduced myself as a journalist and writer. Father Gioele was a warm and friendly character, and he proudly showed me each upgrade made to his beloved church. He went on to inform me that Sant'Andrea Church was the people's church, and as such remained open until midnight; "We keep the church open to make it accessible to all, including shift workers and people who cannot sleep, so that they can come and pray."

I asked if he knew whether the church had ever had a tabernacle.

"Oh, yes, there was a tabernacle, which sadly was not replaced when the church was renovated in 1998. It was very old and not used anymore. It was mounted on the right-hand side as you face the altar. It has now been replaced by a plaque with a commemorative inscription, honouring the priests who served in this church over the years; the plaque was made and donated by a local blacksmith. There is a new tabernacle which now sits on top of the altar, for storing the holy water and wafers, as is the new tradition of many of the churches today."

I thanked Father Gioele for his time and information, and headed back to join Eddie and Olivia.

"Well, folks, this time we have a problem." I went on to update Olivia and Eddie with the information passed on to me by the priest.

We sat in silence, wondering where we go from here.

Eddie broke the silence; “We have two choices: either take what we have and forget about the conspiracy, or find a way of breaking into the church and removing the plaque, to uncover the hidden tabernacle.”

“How do we do that when the church is open ‘til midnight?”

We debated backward and forward for a while, until it was unanimous: we had come so far, and we wanted to know how the story ended. It was a great feeling having discovered so much treasure, but our thirst for the truth was now equally as important to us; we didn’t want to walk away.

We used our previous knowledge to come up with a plan. This time, there was no need to break into Sant’Andrea Church, as the church would be open, but more importantly securing a way out, once inside. We knew that we were going to create a mess before we could uncover the tabernacle, and would come prepared. We planned every minute detail.

We entered the church at 11.30 p.m., giving us thirty minutes to store our tools and find somewhere to hide. Olivia had her usual role of driving us to our destination, and returning to pick us up when she got my call.

Once inside, we sat in the back pew, watching as the last person left.

Our eyes scanned the church and, making sure we were the only two people remaining inside, we made our way to the altar – this was where we intended to hide, until the lights were switched off. When we heard footsteps, then clicking and bolting sounds, we knew we were locked in for the night.

Wasting no time, we picked up our tool bags and began to unscrew the plaque, which was a little more difficult than anticipated. Finally, we had the plaque removed, and carefully placed it on the marble floor, to put it back when finished.

The tabernacle door was missing, and was now bricked up. One by one we carefully removed the bricks.

Once we were through, Eddie looked inside and noticed that even the stonework was removed, leaving just an open space, with a deep cavity to one side. Someone had obviously been here before us, and that someone obviously had the treasure. The question was who?

With nothing to show for our efforts, we stacked the bricks back inside the tabernacle entrance and screwed the plaque back into position.

We made our way over to the altar in silence and sat on the floor, wondering who was in possession of the spoils – and, more importantly, what was the next part of the puzzle.

"I think it's the architect," Eddie said.

"I think it's the priest," I replied.

We both had the same idea, to go and snoop in the vestry, and try to find any evidence to help us. The door was locked, which left us with no alternative than to prise it open with a crowbar, trying to keep the damage as minimal as possible.

We were in luck: the filing cabinets still had the keys in the lock. As we rummaged, we came across a section headed *"1998 Renovations"*, with sub-dividers for invoices, plans and expenses. We didn't have anything else to do, so we made ourselves comfortable and each took a section at a time to look through.

There was a section on the work carried out on the tabernacle; this included various sketches of plaques and clearly illustrated the plaque which had been chosen, with estimates and invoices for the work to be completed, written on paper headed: *"Lorenzo and Sons Blacksmith Company, Montevarchi."* We now had the name and whereabouts of the blacksmith.

Our brains must have been frazzled; why did we not think of

the blacksmith in the first place? He must surely be suspect number one!

We closed the vestry doors as best we could, and headed back to our hiding place behind the altar, with another two hours before the church opened.

At seven o'clock we heard the doors opening. We waited silently, until it was once again soundless, before peeping our heads out from behind the altar, to make sure there was no one there. Once assured it was safe to leave, we headed for the doors and made our exit.

We called Olivia to come and get us, letting her know that we would be standing outside the train station.

"You could both do with a shower and a change of clothes," were the first words Olivia muttered to us.

"I thought women liked natural male pheromones."

"Not this strong, Nathan."

When we returned home, we took Olivia's hint and spruced ourselves up.

After a light snack, we told Olivia what had happened.

It was a given that we needed to pay the blacksmith a visit.

We took a drive back to Montevarchi, straight to the address written on the blacksmith's invoice.

We were in luck: the workshop was open; we could see a man in his seventies tinkering away at a forge.

Eddie brought out a fake I.D. card and flashed it quickly under the blacksmith's nose. Suited and booted, we looked every bit the part of Vatican agents, sent to investigate missing inventories and treasures which were stored in various churches throughout Italy. We asked if he was the owner, and if he was the person who made and installed the plaque at the Sant'Andrea a Cennano Church.

Lorenzo, the elderly blacksmith, was trying to stall, and before he had time to contrive an answer, I asked if I could use the *banio*, at the same time proceeding inside without an answer, on the pretence of using the facilities. The blacksmith followed me inside, with Eddie quick on his tail.

Framed on the wall, above a metal shelf, there was a small wooden door, which very much resembled that of a tabernacle. Pointing to the wooden door, I continued to interrogate the old boy: "What else did you take that day? Be careful how you answer, because if you are part of the gang that stole from churches all over Italy – which a God-fearing man will know belong to the Vatican – you will be looking at spending the rest of your life behind bars."

He slumped into a chair and held his head in his hands. "I am a hard-working blacksmith with one son, two daughters and a wife, who has suffered for years with arthritis. I have been the sole provider of my family for more years than I can remember. I saw this as an opportunity and, sadly, took the treasure. Oh, My God, please forgive me and have mercy on me. You must believe me when I say I know nothing about other churches; I am not part of any gang."

Eddie glanced over at me, with a look seeming to question where we go from here. I, on the other hand, remained in character.

"Why should we believe you? Just give us the names of the other members of the gang, and we will be lenient on you."

Eddie gestured with raised hands, as if to say: "What are you doing?"

I came back to Earth. "Okay, old man, we believe you. Just tell us what you have done with the treasure."

The old boy asked: "Will I still be in trouble if I give you what I have?"

Eddie looked at me and shrugged his shoulders, as if to

gesture that it was my call.

I answered the old boy: "It will decrease the chances of you going to prison, that's for sure."

Without any hesitation, the blacksmith replied: "Okay." He slowly walked over to the corner of the room, where there was a large plant, at least two metres tall and a metre in circumference. He asked if I could remove the plant pot from the large ornate vase it stood inside, which I did. He bent down to pull out a second aluminium plant holder, and handed me an envelope from within.

Inside the envelope was a red pouch, containing various jewels and a letter. I asked Eddie to check the contents of the pouch against "the list", and tell me what was missing.

At this, the old man was very forthcoming, and made our job easier by offloading as quickly as he could; "Sir, I can tell you exactly what's missing: a diamond-studded brooch in the shape of a star and five gold medallions."

Eddie wrote on a piece of paper and passed it to me. The note read: *"Ask him if he knows how much the five gold medallions and the diamond-studded brooch would be worth today."*

I asked the old man the question, to which he replied: "About sixty-five-thousand euros, but I swear I only got a total of twenty-thousand euros."

I handed the blacksmith a piece of paper, listing the items we were taking away, and asked him to sign it, while Eddie looked at me with no words spoken. We then wanted to leave Lorenzo to enjoy the rest of his life.

Before leaving, I wanted to give the old boy some reassurance that nobody else would be bothering him, as long as he kept this meeting confidential. "We believe that you had no further involvement; it is the gang the Vatican are interested in. We will put in a good word for you, and explain that the missing items may have been already removed by one of the gang members, before you took the pouch."

The blacksmith was so relieved that we were not going to take the matter further, and promised that he would make a generous donation to the church, to atone for his sins. We nodded as if to say we approved of his intentions. Then, taking the remaining treasure and the wooden tabernacle door as "evidence", we bade Lorenzo goodbye.

"Grazi milli," he whispered, as we left.

On the way back to Terranuova, I stopped the car and parked in a layby. My mind was troubled and Eddie could sense it.

"What's troubling you, mate?"

Trying to put the pieces together, I replied: "Are we out of our depth with this? I'm worried. What if Father Gioele reported this to the Vatican? It's possible that they could be carrying out the same investigations we are; they would never make it public that there was a conspiracy within the Church, even if it was centuries ago.

"My thoughts also keep going back to my cousin Roberto, and what he said to me: '*I think Agostino was murdered!*' Where do we go from here?"

Eddie looked at me and said: "Nathan, I've had the same thoughts, mate. We have two choices: we can stop our search, bite the bullet, forget about the conspiracy and go back to England, or we can take our chances and follow it through to the end. You decide."

Chapter 17

I started to think of our Cardinal Bertocelli. If he was living in Terranuova, surely people would have brought their treasures to him as and when an opportunity arose, meaning that he would have had to live close to the piazza.

I remembered one of the letters stating something about leaving the church doors open: *"I will keep the back door open from 9.00 p.m. to 10.00 p.m. on the last Monday of each month, until our mission is completed..."* There must have been some sort of vault, where the money and treasure were stored, until needed to exchange for favours or weapons. The main treasury was right under our noses! There was now no doubt in my mind that Terranuova held the key to the majority of the missing pieces.

It was Friday, so we decided to take a stroll around the various market stalls which frequented the piazza every week. Olivia walked between me and Eddie, laughing and joking about no particular subject. Just for today we were locals enjoying our town.

Olivia wanted to buy some of the many cheeses and delicacies of the region, and decisively stated: “I think a light lunch, washed down with the bottle of Rocca Guelfa we purchased when we visited San Gimignano, would be perfect for a day like this.”

“Sounds delicious,” me and Eddie replied in stereo.

The market stallholder called out: “Chi è il prossimo *(Who's next)*?” Simultaneously, me and another guy held up our baskets.

“After you,” said the old man.

Then, as his eyes met with mine, he looked shocked, as if frozen in time; the old man seemed to recognize me – from where, I had no idea. When his eyes quickly darted from mine to Eddie's, I could sense that he was becoming more and more guarded and uncomfortable.

Without disagreement, I handed the basket to the market stallholder, made my payment and left. As we walked away, I realized who the old man was – which, in turn, made me uncomfortable, too.

“You're very quiet,” Eddie said, before adding; “what's wrong?”

I explained that Lorenzo the blacksmith was here in the square, and that I was sure he had recognized us.

“Oh, come on, Nathan, even if he had, why would he want to

bring trouble to his door? You saw how quick he squealed when we paid him a visit. I don't think we have anything to worry about."

I wished I had Eddie's optimism, but my gut feeling told me to stay alert.

Eddie was meeting up with Gianna, which always seemed to put him in a good mood; I was starting to think that this could be "the one" for him. Better take my best suit to the dry cleaners!

I watched Lorenzo walk away from the piazza, and checked that no one was following us before returning home. There was not much I could do about the situation, so I decided to concentrate on the last church on the list, according to the maps and documents we had managed to uncover.

Terranuova was my home town, and it felt a tad as if I was betraying my neighbours and friends, breaking into the local church. If this was the last church, surely it would reveal not only a larger share of the spoils, but maybe damaging proof of the conspiracy plotted – after all, this was the church which Cardinal Bertocelli used for supporters of the cause to deliver their contributions.

I wondered where he stayed when he visited Terranuova; in my mind, I was sure it had to be nearby. Was this another coincidence, or was I fated to be the one to uncover what Cardinal Bertocelli and his merry men were plotting against England and King Henry VIII? The more I thought about it, the more I started to believe that Cardinal Bertocelli may have been dwelling in my very own home, the house that my nono Agostino had lived in for most of his life, and ultimately died in. How much did my nono know? I wished I had a crystal ball; but it seemed I would have to wait until each new piece of evidence uncovered revealed a little more.

Back home, the television was on, but my thoughts were elsewhere, working overtime.

Cardinal Bertocelli would have needed the aid of the local authoritarians for such a task. Many years ago, the authoritarians held the same power as that held by the Mafia in the 1960s; such people would have knowledge of who to contact, if help was needed to store items with no questions asked. The authoritarians would have considered providing their support in these matters as an honour, to help the priesthood. I had so many thoughts swirling around in my head, and so many unanswered questions.

I needed to switch off, so once Olivia's programme had finished, we decided to dress up and take a stroll back into town. We chose a charming, family-run local restaurant to dine in. It was just what the doctor ordered: a chance to refresh the body and mind before our research continued.

*

Although it turned into a pretty late night, we were up early and, after a light breakfast, spent the rest of the morning unscrambling more of the documentation given to us by Lorenzo.

The map in my hand was exactly the same as all the others, and I was beginning to feel that there was no more to uncover. There was, however, one notable difference between this map and the previous ones: this map had an elaborate border. Why would anybody go to such efforts? The border was adorned with interwinding red vines, encrusted in gold leaf, and although I could not yet see the reason for this extravagance, I felt that the fancy work was intended to tell the reader to look deeper. Picking up the magnifying glass from the side table, I inspected closer the ornate border.

I could see individual letters concealed within the pattern. I wrote down every letter – twelve in total – but I knew that it would take me twice as long as Olivia to work out what they represented.

"Olivia, I know how much you enjoy anagrams. Can you

create a word from these letters?"

"No problem. Pour me a glass of fresh orange juice, with a splash of cranberry and lots of crushed ice, and I'll take a look." Taking the piece of paper from my hand, she made herself comfortable and eagerly started to play around with the letters. "Nathan, can you pass me the map, too? I think it might give a hint to the order in which the letters need to be arranged."

There followed a period of studious silence.

Olivia broke it: "Who's Biagio ai Mori?"

I shook my head and gave her a big smile, before saying: "You clever woman! Now we just have to figure out who Biagio ai Mori was!"

Olivia looked pleased with herself, and was keen to solve the mystery. "Pass me the books I picked up from the library and my laptop. I'm sure between us we will find the answer." Olivia had a bit between her teeth now; she was not going to give up until she had cracked the code.

Within minutes of scanning and cross-referencing, she shouted: "Biagio ai Mori is not a person; it's a church in Terranuova. It says here: *'The Church of San Biagio was built in the new walled village around the middle of the 14th century, by the people of the Moors, who dedicated it to San Biagio and*

San Paolo.'" Olivia showed me pictures of the church, which I instantly recognized.

"I know that church! It's the one opposite the car park, at the end of our road."

"I think I deserve a treat for cracking the conundrum!"

I gave her a big kiss and told her that she could choose how we spent the evening.

Olivia gave me a saucy grin and said: "Really?"

By the time we left home it was late afternoon. We decided to visit San Biagio, as it was only a five-minute walk away.

On the way there, I was shaking my head with a smile. Olivia asked what was amusing me.

"I was so convinced that the final church would be the one in the piazza. Just shows that it's not always the most obvious choice."

"Well, hello," a voice interrupted us. "Where are you two going?" It was Eddie, who had apparently run out of coffee.

"Where's Gianna? Still in bed?"

"No, Nathan, we're not teenagers. She's gone to work."

Olivia looked at me and asked him: "Do you want to join us?"

"Are you sure I'm not playing gooseberry?"

I replied: "Of course not. *We're* not teenagers!"

San Biagio looked inconspicuous, situated between dwellings, directly opposite a car park. The round window above the panelled walnut doors, and the stone pillars on either side of the frontage, were the only giveaway signs that this was not a residential occupancy. The building was painted in a washed-out sandstone colour, which had seen better days, and the paving stones in front of the church were also in need of restoration. San Biagio ai Mori was very unassuming.

Unfortunately, my assumption that churches were open on Saturdays proved to be wrong, and the door was locked.

A lady walking past asked if we needed help. We asked her what time the church opened, and were surprised to be told that it no longer opened for services. The lady went on to explain that the locals had been trying to get the church reopened for many years, to no avail. However, the priest who held services in Santa Maria, in the main piazza, also held the keys to this church. The lady proudly went on to say how Father Luca was very attached to San Biagio, as this was where he began his calling, many years ago, and added that Father Luca was proud to show visitors and residents of the town his beloved church.

We made a rendezvous to meet the priest after the six o'clock service at Santa Maria.

He was older than the average priest, and spent what seemed an age nattering to his congregation, before walking over to where we sat, patiently waiting for him. After making his apologies, we followed Father Luca to San Biagio ai Mori.

He proudly opened the church doors and started to tell us the history of some of the frescos decorating the inside walls. I asked for permission to take photos, which was received gratefully, with a hand gesture and a nod to stamp his approval. Father Luca was soon in full flow, updating us with his knowledge that the church was built in the 5th century, and how it had undertaken restoration in both the 5th and 7th centuries. He continued to explain how the nave and vaulted ceilings were added in the first restoration, and in the second a cupola above the high altar was included. With clear passion, Father Luca gave us the history of the frescos, offering greatest adulation to the most ancient, which was painted in 1385 and represented Saint Anthony Abbott, Saint Michael Archangel, Saint Peter and Saint Lucia. He went on to date and describe the other cycle, dated 1388, which included figures of "the Virgin enthroned with child" and Saint John the Baptist, Blaise and Bartholomew.

We thanked Father Luca for his hospitality and, after dropping a small donation into the wooden box, made our way to the entrance of the church. We watched while Father Luca locked up, and I gave a sigh as the thought process began once again to swirl around in my mind.

"Have you worked out how we get in?" Eddie asked.

Apprehensively, I replied: "I think we need to give this some serious thought."

We made our way home, lost in our individual thoughts, and very much aware that this was bringing us nearer to the end of our journey.

San Biagio ai Mori was not going to be an easy target. It had no back or side entrance; the only way in was through the main doors at the front of the church.

It went against my grain to break into a church on my own doorstep; breaking the silence, I muttered: "I don't think I can do it, Eddie. It doesn't feel right."

We spent the next few weeks mulling over where to go from here. Should we just get rid of what we already had, going back to Hendrik and selling the lot, to lead normal lives? Or should we finish what we started?

I knew I couldn't leave this unsolved.

It took a further week before I cracked it.

"Eddie, we're going to fix the church!" I exclaimed.

"Are you feeling okay? What planet are you on now?" Eddie responded.

At last, the answer to our progression was in my grasp. I knew that the only way to gain access was to make Father Luca an offer he could surely not refuse. We were going to redecorate his church.

"What reason will you give for us redecorating the church?" Olivia piped in. "After all, no services are held there anymore. If the church has no purpose, why would Father Luca agree to this work; what benefit would it serve?"

"Olivia, what if we gave him a reason for reopening his beloved historical church?"

"I'm intrigued," Eddie conceded.

I spent the next few days putting together a proposal to present to Father Luca. I wanted this to be a winning situation for Terranuova, San Biagio and us. At last, a credible plan was completed.

Olivia and Eddie scrutinized the proposal and, after adding a little and subtracting a little, we were ready to make another appointment with Father Luca.

Olivia popped out to get a few bits for lunch. On her return, she casually mentioned that two men had asked if she was a local, as they were lost. Olivia went on to tell us how pleased she was to be taken for a local, but explained to them that she had only moved to the area recently, so unfortunately could not help.

After the encounter with Lorenzo the day before, I felt a little uneasy. "What did they look like?" I asked, in a nonchalant fashion.

"Oh, you know, average build, dark hair, Mediterranean colouring and features. Not bad looking, if you like that sort. Why, are you jealous?"

"I just find it strange that anyone would mistake you for a local." I thought about adding that I had felt, on a few occasions, that we had been followed, but I didn't want to spook Olivia unnecessarily.

"As a precaution, I just think we should all be vigilant and take no unnecessary chances."

Eddie returned just in time for a quick coffee, before our rendezvous with the priest. We had made arrangements to meet Father Luca that afternoon, and hoped that our plan would be welcomed.

Upon our arrival, the vestry looked like it needed updating, and Father Luca apologized for not being able to offer us any sort of refreshment, due to the lack of working facilities. God must have been on my side, as this actually gave me my opening line:

"Well, we may be able to help with this matter, Father. After our last visit with you, we went away wishing that we could help restore the church – at least to a standard which would enable it to once again be used for special occasions and services."

Father Luca's eyes widened with enthusiasm. "We have three churches within close proximity to San Biagio ai Mori, and for this reason our town council will not fund the work needed to restore this humble but historical church. You know, in its days this church was graced with many important men of the cloth – even Cardinal Bertocelli."

My eyes met Eddie's, and I knew he was thinking the same as me; we could almost sense the Cardinal's presence.

Father Luca went on to explain that he and his parishioners had tried to cover the costs, but even after years of donations from one fundraiser or another, they would need at least the same amount again to commence work. He concluded by saying: "I thank you for your offer, but unfortunately I will not be able to pay you for your labour, and only a small amount toward materials."

I explained to him: "I don't think you understand, Father; we want to do this as an anonymous gift."

Father Luca looked at us in utter disbelief. After raising his hands to the ceiling and thanking God for this blessing, he asked why we wanted to do this.

I answered unhesitantly; it was as if the reason for doing this was there before the opportunity had even arisen: "I want to do this in honour of my nono, who was born in this village, baptized in this church and married here, many years ago."

Father Luca could not thank us enough, and could not hide his excitement at the prospect of performing services, like in the years gone by.

I explained that the first stage would be to draw up an itinerary, so that we would know what we needed and how much it would cost to carry out the essential work, before moving on to the second stage: adding the furnishings, to make it a place where people could come and sit, pray and hopefully enjoy special occasions, once again.

We shook hands and I asked Father Luca if this made him happy, to which he replied: "Happy is an understatement! I cannot thank you both enough for your generosity. Your nono must have been very special to you. I must know him, if he was baptized and married at San Biagio; what is his name?"

"Agostino Mancini."

Chapter 18

Olivia had left me a note to say that she was popping into the local shops for a few bits and bobs, and that there was plenty in the fridge for a snack, if I couldn't wait until tonight. I made myself a coffee and grabbed a few biscotti to tide me over.

Olivia had left paperwork sprawled across the coffee table and, as I made myself comfortable, I noticed an A4 sheet with Olivia's writing, and a copy of a letter written in Latin attached to it:

"Carus Bertocelli,

Nuntium dictum, quam diu res haberet quo progreditur. Et pecuniam necessarium tibi laborantes populi legatione perfectum est visus. Suspendisse quis speravit in pauca mihi curae nostrae conversionis nostrae pecuniae opere commutato. Placere instruere pergemus: ubi obviam ad disceptandum tenuiores details. Habui breviter nunc vero sentio, necessitas quaedam particularia transire vobiscum.

Vestra humilis amicus,

Antonio."

It seemed that Olivia had managed to translate another letter. Taking a sip of coffee, I started to read:

"My dearest Cardinal Bertocelli,

It has been a while since we have had any news on how things are progressing. Your people have worked hard and the necessary funds to complete our mission are in sight. I have a few trusted men in our syndicate who will be responsible for undertaking the task of converting our treasure into money. Please instruct where we will meet to discuss the finer details. I have kept this brief for now, however, I do feel the need to go over certain particulars with you.

Your humble and loyal friend,

Antonio."

I wondered who Antonio could be.

I had read how the struggle for supremacy in Italy between France and Spain was resolved, in favour of Spain. Caught between the Spanish-Imperial and Turkish superpowers, the

Republic adopted a skilful political strategy of quasi-neutrality in Europe, which turned into a defensive stance against the Ottomans. Venice's maritime aid was potentially useful to Spain, but not to the point of allowing her to reinforce her position in the Levant, which would increase her strength in Italy as well, where she was practically the only Italian state not subject to Spain. In the Turkish war of 1537-40, Venice was allied with the emperor and king of Spain, Charles V. Andrea Doria, commander of the allied fleets, was defeated at Preveza in 1538, and two years later Venice signed a treaty of peace, by which the Turks took the Aegean duchy of Naxos from the Sanudo family. After Preveza, the supremacy of the sea passed to the Ottomans.

Difficulties in the rule of the sea brought further changes. Until 1545, the oarsmen in the galleys were free sailors enrolled on a wage. They were originally Venetians, but later Dalmatians, Cretans and Greeks joined in large numbers. Because of the difficulty in hiring sufficient crews, Venice had recourse to conscription, chaining the oarsmen to the benches, as other navies had already done. Cristoforo Da Canal was the first Venetian to command such a galley. By 1563, the population of Venice had dropped to about 168,000 people.

This raised a question regarding Antonio: was he Italian,

French or Spanish?

I could hear Olivia in the kitchen.

"You're back," I called. "I was going to send out a search party! What have you been buying?"

"Oh, a bit of this and a bit of that," Olivia replied, as she was placing a wrapped parcel in a drawer. I guessed she didn't want me to know what she was hiding, so I didn't let on that I saw.

We invited Eddie and Gianna over for a bite to eat; it was good that the girls got on so well. Later that evening, me and Eddie took a stroll, and ended outside San Biagio ai Mori.

Father Luca had given me a set of keys earlier that day and, checking that nobody was about, I took the keys out of my pocket and opened the doors. Once inside, we sat together on one of the worn-out pews, just us and our thoughts.

Within minutes, we heard the door opening.

"Eddie, didn't you lock the doors?" I whispered.

"I thought you did," he whispered back.

Slowly, we turned around to see who was there. Two men were walking toward the pew directly opposite us.

I would bet my last penny that these were the same two men who had asked Olivia for directions.

I did not want them to suspect that we were concerned, so I

casually turned toward them and said: "Sorry, guys, the church is closed for renovations; we're only here to meet up with the local surveyor and his team. They should be here any moment." I was making it clear there was going to be company on its way.

Without as much as a goodbye, they acknowledged us with a nod and left. My suspicions were growing; someone was onto us.

"Phew," said Eddie, as he grabbed the keys from my hand and locked the doors. "I knew we were being followed. Now we need to work out why and who they are."

My mind tried to block out our new problem for the moment, by concentrating on the here and now. "Eddie, the last time we were here I noticed that some work had been carried out inside the sacristy."

"Nathan, can you speak English? What in Heaven's name is a sacristy?"

"It's where the priest and his entourage keep their garments, to change into and prepare before a service. It's also where they return at the end of the service, to remove their clothing and put away any of the sacred vessels and church objects used during a service. Some churches even keep their parish registers there, for safekeeping."

"I'm impressed! When did you become so clued up on the Church? Of course, you could have called it the 'vestry' and saved me the lesson." We both laughed.

Making sure we securely locked the church, we went back to join the girls. We left none the wiser, my mind drifting back to the two men who followed us into the church. The only thing we identified tonight was that the tabernacle was empty, and further inspection did not reveal any signs of a false cavity wall, either.

"Eddie this time the tabernacle has no bearings on the treasure. One thing's for sure: there cannot be a false wall; the tabernacle has been built on an outside wall, so it can't possibly have a cavity."

We watched Eddie and Gianna walk back across the Piazza; I poured a drink and stared out of the window, looking, I supposed, to see if our buddies were lurking. The piazza was quieter than usual tonight, not even disturbed by last-minute shoppers making their way home; no locals standing making polite chit chat; and thankfully no sign of our stalkers.

Olivia put her arms around my waist and rested her head on my back. "Penny for your thoughts," she said.

"Just thinking, that's all." I turned and kissed her softly, and it wasn't long before all the concerns of the day were banished.

The next few days were spent putting together a list of the work needing attention. There was going to be more than I could take on by myself; scaffolding would need to be erected both externally and internally. Contractors, from plasterers to carpenters to roofers, would need to be hired, and suppliers identified to purchase materials. All of this needed to be considered, as well as ensuring that either myself, Eddie or both of us would need to be on site at all times, in the event of our restoration uncovering Cardinal Bertocelli's stash. I drew up the plans and began to list the funds required.

A visit to my cousin Marco was necessary – he, after all, was the man with all the right (and not so right) connections. I gave him a quick call.

"Ciao, Marco, it's Nathan. When is a good time for me to come round? I need your help in a new project I'm undertaking."

"I'm home all day today, so whenever it suits you, my uomo Inglese." Marco still referred to me as the English man. "Are you bringing your lovely Olivia with you, or are you coming alone?"

"I'm coming alone, Marco. That way we won't be distracted."

I took a shower and put on some casuals. Then, kissing Olivia goodbye, I headed over to Marco's.

It was a beautiful day, so I decided to walk. For me, walking was always the best remedy for mulling things over. Besides, it gave me time to breathe in my hometown, with its locals chit-chatting and the church bells ringing on the hour.

Was I becoming paranoid, or was I being followed? I could almost sense somebody walking behind me.

I turned, trying not to look too conspicuous, and noticed one suspicious-looking man across the road... and, yes, another behind me. They very much resembled the two guys who had followed me and Eddie into the church a few days ago.

Not wanting to imperil Marco and his family, I gave Marco a call and arranged to meet him at The Jolly Bar in Via Roma.

I took a seat outside, facing the window, so that I could see the reflections of people walking by. My fears were confirmed when I saw one of the guys signal to the other, then disappear down one of the side roads.

Marco arrived shortly and, after the usual hugs and greetings, we ordered salami and mozzarella paninis and cold beers.

"Are you okay? Why the sudden change of rendezvous?"

"Marco, where do I begin? I have so much to tell you, but at this stage I just need you to trust me; all will be revealed to you in good time."

"You have it, my friend. What do you need?"

I showed Marco the plans for the renovations to San Biagio Church in Terranuova.

Marco carefully considered the amount of manpower a project like this would need, so he could accurately gauge how many employees to hire. He also listed which were the best suppliers to purchase materials from, and where they were located. Marco was an expert in this field, and made light work of my long list, by making just one single phone call to a well-known associate, who had a whole team of reliable and experienced traders working for him. Marco didn't ask any questions as to where the money to fund this project was coming from, and I didn't feel the need to say anymore. Marco arranged for his associate Andreas to meet me at his house tomorrow, at three o'clock. I could tell by Marco's responses that Andreas was pleased for the work.

"Marco, I have another small problem, which I may need to call on you for support, but at the moment I think I can handle it." I didn't want to worry Marco more than necessary, but I needed the reassurance that he was available if needed at short notice.

"Just call anytime, Nathan, night or day; it's no problem."

I took a different route back home, paying extra attention to my surroundings.

I used the shop windows to observe reflections, and it wasn't long before my two stalkers were spotted. My hunch was that they already knew where I lived – after all, they had been following me for some time – so I decided to go straight home.

Once in, double-checking that the door was bolted, I headed up the stairs, where Olivia was watching some chat show, which happened to be showing in English. I looked out of the window facing the piazza, and could see the back of the two men walking away. My instinct told me that they were not sent to harm me at this stage, but to gather information.

With that in mind, the rest of the evening was spent enjoying some winding-down time.

After yesterday's fiasco, I decided to drive over to Marco's for my meeting with Andreas, checking in the mirror for any signs of being followed – sure enough, there was a black Lancia on my tail.

On arrival, I switched off the engine and watched the black Lancia drive slowly past me. I got out of the car and observed the driver and his passenger, driving on in a manner not to bring any attention to themselves.

Andreas was already inside, sipping what looked like a double espresso. Marco introduced us and, after the greetings were exchanged, we sat down to business. I gave Andreas a copy of the plans, and we decided to take a trip to San Biagio Church, for Andreas to add any additional notes.

Thinking ahead, to avoid being followed I suggested leaving my car at Marco's, and for us to drive to Terranuova in Andreas's car. With all in agreement, we made our way to San Biagio.

With pencil and notepad in hand, Andreas asked questions about materials and styles I wanted to use, documenting my requests. I showed him what needed to be done, and asked him to provide me with a breakdown of the cost for both materials and labour. Andreas pointed out that this may come to a little more than a standard commercial building, as in addition to skilled carpenters, painters, restorers and general labourers, there would be the need to hire an expert surveyor from the council, because of the history and antiquity of the building. With this in mind, I asked Andreas to include the expense of hiring a surveyor in the total cost. Once everything was noted and a timespan agreed, we made arrangements for Andreas to contact me, as soon as possible, with the final prices.

Marco asked if I wanted to come back with them, or would rather pick the car up at my leisure. The latter seemed a good idea so, saying goodbye to both, I made my way back on foot.

*

I received a phone call from Marco very early the next morning.

"Nathan, your small problem, has it anything to do with two men in a black Lancia?"

"Why do you ask?" I said, sitting up.

"Because they are sitting in the car outside, right now, watching my house."

I paused for a moment, then said: "I think you'd better come over." Marco agreed.

While we were waiting for Marco's arrival, I took the opportunity to tell Olivia the potential danger we were facing, then called Eddie to come over as soon as he could.

I had enough time to update Eddie with what had been going on. After much discussion, Eddie and Olivia agreed that it was sensible to bring Marco into the picture.

When we were all present, Olivia made us double espressos and served the coffees with small pastries from the local patisserie.

I proceeded to tell Marco everything, and he listened in astonishment.

"Where have you been storing this treasure?" Marco asked.

We all stood up and, leading the way, I took Marco to reveal what we had uncovered. He watched as Eddie and I moved the washing machine forward, silently wondering what we were going to reveal.

"Come into our secret room."

Stepping inside, Marco's eyes widened in bewilderment.

"Are you okay?" I asked.

"I have never seen such a collection in one place! And, you say you have sold a substantial amount already?! Nathan, so many questions are running through my mind at the moment. Who else knows about this, my friend, and how many people have your contacts spoken to? The amount of security you will need depends on who you sold the goods to."

I shrugged my shoulders and said: "Marco, I'm not a private dick; how am I supposed to know? Me and Eddie have done our hardest not to attract too much attention, but all I can say, hand on heart, is that our connections in Antwerp do not know where we acquired our goods – or even where we live, for that matter."

"Well, Nathan, they do know what country you are in, so how quickly they will track you down depends only on how well connected they are."

Marco and I decided to take a stroll, to talk more. Eddie thought it would be a good idea if he sat in the cafeteria across the road, where he could see if anyone of interest was visiting our village. We walked to the bottom of the road and sat down in a small café near the bus station.

Marco took a notepad out of his jacket pocket and said: "Nathan, I need a list of all the people you have been in contact with, regarding the jewels and the documents you found."

I started reeling off names. "Well, as I already told you, there's the blacksmith Lorenzo, who me and Eddie had to pay a visit to. Then there's Fredrik and Hendrik, in Antwerp." I held my head in my hands, trying hard to think of anybody else. "At this moment I think that's it: just the blacksmith over here and Fredrik and Hendrik abroad."

"Okay, Nathan. I will speak to your old buddies in the red Alfa and have them reassigned as your bodyguards. Their first assignment will be to find out who the two men in the black Lancia are – and, more importantly, who hired them. Then, we have the matter of the blacksmith Lorenzo to deal with, as well as anybody he has spoken with. This is big, Nathan; I think you will need heavy protection. And we need to have a backup plan."

"I'm not leaving Italy, Marco; any backup plan has to take this into consideration. Although my priority is Olivia's safety, I don't want to take her back to England unless it's absolutely necessary. There must be a way to keep her safe without her having to go back. As for Eddie, I'm sure he will also want to stay in Italy – for more than one reason."

It felt like a heavy weight had been lifted from my shoulders, knowing that Marco was now in on the plan. Offloading everything to him was better than going to confession. Feeling lighter, I bade Marco goodnight and headed home.

On the way back I spotted Eddie still sitting in the cafeteria, and waved over to him. He came out to chat, and to inform me that all was quiet on the home front.

"I'm going to grab an overnight bag and stay at Gianna's tonight. If you need me, send a text and I'll get straight back to you."

I headed inside and upstairs, yelling out: "Honey, I'm home."

She seemed preoccupied and gave no response, so I asked: "Olivia, what's up? Are you okay?"

There was a pause, before Olivia asked: "How long will we have to live under surveillance? This is beginning to scare me."

"I don't know. I just know that I'm committed to finishing what we started; there's no going back for me. I want you here with me, but I could not live with myself if I was the cause of anything happening to you. So, if you want to go back then we'll make it happen, and as soon as it's all over you can come back."

Olivia held two fingers against my lips and said: "I don't want to leave. I'm just worried, that's all."

I gave her a long, firm squeeze and tried to make her feel safe again. None of this mattered if Olivia was not here, and I wanted her to know that I would never put her life at risk.

Getting ready to meet Andreas, I asked Olivia if she wanted to come along, as I didn't want her feeling trapped in the house, and I didn't want her going out by herself.

"I think that's a good idea," she agreed. "I could do with some fresh air."

We ordered a round of non-alcoholic refreshments and an assortment of appetisers to nibble on, while we waited for Andreas to join us. I saw that my bodyguards were already parked in view across the road.

Andreas was on foot. He walked over to where we were sitting and, after I introduced him to Olivia, we settled down to business.

I was impressed: the man knew his stuff, and the cost for materials, taking into consideration which grade of materials were going to be used, were similar to my reckoning. Andreas told me that Marco had called him, to ask if he could make this job on San Biagio Church a priority; I was doubly impressed when Andreas went on to say that, after rearranging a few contracts, he could start work tomorrow.

We shook hands and arranged to meet at the bank, so that a small token deposit could be transferred to Andreas's account.

Next morning, Andreas turned up with a handful of men, in a van loaded with scaffolding equipment.

After dropping the men off at the church, Andreas and I went to the local bank, followed by a trip to the council, to log the work at San Biagio Church. This was followed by a visit to the local surveyor's office, to arrange a survey and all other legalities required for a historical building.

Afterward, I shook Andreas's hand and left the restoration project in his capable hands. I reminded him that he would mainly be working with Eddie on a day-to-day basis, with me taking Eddie's place when he was not around. I did not want Andreas to feel that he was not trusted, and reassured him that the only reason this was necessary was because the person commissioning the work gave strict instructions that one of us must be on site while it is being carried out. I managed to convince Andreas that this was the only reason for us being present daily and, by his nod, I could see that this was acceptable to him.

As I walked in, Marco called to update me with news about our two guys in the black Lancia. Not wanting to share his information over the phone, Marco said that he would be over in half an hour.

Straight away, I called to ask Eddie to come over. He was still at Gianna's, but by coincidence was just leaving, and should be with me in less than ten minutes.

Olivia was studiously catching up with her translations as I stared out of the window, waiting anxiously for Marco. When Marco and Eddie arrived, Olivia made her excuses to retreat to the bedroom, adding that she had letters which needed replying to.

I poured Eddie and Marco a drink, then both me and Eddie looked at Marco nervously.

Finally, he spoke: "Your friends in the Lancia are Vatican agents, sent to investigate two men posing as police officers instructed by the Vatican, regarding stolen articles which belong to them. Does this sound familiar, my friends?"

"Mamma mia! Where did they get their information from?" Eddie exclaimed.

Marco enlightened us that a blacksmith named Lorenzo had made a call to the Vatican. "And the rest, my friends, you know."

Eddie looked at me. "What are we gonna do?"

I shrugged my shoulders and looked at Marco, knowing now that this was going to start getting ugly.

"Let's just say you won't be seeing the two guys or their black Lancia anymore," he said, quietly.

I was horrified by the implication. "Marco, you can't just get rid of two Vatican agents without attracting more attention."

"Believe me, my friends, when I do a job I do it thoroughly. Without leaving any sign of a break-in, my men have gained access to computers, diaries, photographs and other incriminating evidence, and have had the lot destroyed. As for the two guys, they met with a terrible accident, and it may take a while to prove the identity of the bodies in the wreck. This gives us sufficient time to pay our friend Lorenzo a visit, before continuing our clean-up operation. But this is nothing for you to worry about."

We were now part of a murder enquiry, which felt more like a mobster movie, with me and Eddie playing the main roles – and my cousin was telling us not to worry! My thoughts were spiralling out of control. What would Olivia think? Was it wrong to keep this from her? I had questions; hundreds of questions. But, if life had taught me anything, it was that lies and wrongdoing had a way of catching up with you.

Marco bade us ciao and reiterated for us not to concern ourselves with the blacksmith, or any other issue relating to this matter.

Eddie left shortly after Marco did, saying that he was going to stay at Gianna's again.

"Two nights in a row," I teased; "must be getting serious!"

"Maybe, but I must say I am glad for the distraction, mate."

Olivia had fallen asleep, and in a way I was glad, as I now didn't have to lie about our conversation tonight.

I joined her in bed and tried to sleep, but this proved difficult.

Although our two buddies in the Lancia were taken care of, it was a certainty that others were involved. I was a businessman, a builder and restorer of furniture, not a killer.

My inner voice started to rationalize the situation: *Wait a minute, we are not the bad guys; we were just chosen, in some way, to uncover the story behind this conspiracy. We were not the ones planning to overthrow the English Monarchy, or plotting to get rid of King Henry VIII.*

Of course, that didn't take away the fact that two men were dead because of me. I started to question who I was becoming.

The conflict continued in my head, and I consoled myself by believing that, if it was not me and Eddie, it would have been somebody else.

I felt better with this rationale and, with a clear conscience, fell into a deep sleep.

*

The next day, I met up with Eddie and Andreas outside the church, as planned.

After a little discussion, we left Andreas to organize his team of workers and headed to the vestry, where Eddie got busy looking for any signs of concealed passages.

In the middle of a gruelling day, we took a break and came across some plasterwork which had been added at a later stage. We looked at each other and, with a nod, each grabbed a bolster and chisel, and began to remove some of the plaster, then some of the bricks, which soon gave way to a dark hole.

I grabbed a torch and shone it into the new space we had uncovered. I could see a stairway.

Removing more bricks, I stepped through the gap to investigate further.

"Shall I lock the vestry door?"

"Good thinking, Eddie; we don't want Andreas or any of the others coming this way."

The stairway led us below the church foundations. We found ourselves in a crypt wandering amongst stone sarcophagi, which spooked both of us.

"Eddie, this feels eerie. To think that there are bodies in these caskets," I whispered, as if anyone could hear us down here.

Eddie turned to face me and said: "But, then again, what a good place to bury treasure!"

We started to slowly open each stone coffin, but found them all empty.

"Why would anyone brick up a crypt full of empty coffins?

What are we missing?"

I asked Eddie to come for a few drinks that evening and chat. There was another matter troubling me. It was not going to be easy, asking my friend to make a choice, but it had to be done.

Before I could get the words out, Eddie made it easy for me: "I've been waiting for you to bring up my relationship with Gianna, mate. I know that I will have to make a painful decision; I don't want to jeopardize our mission. So, before things get any more serious between us, I have decided to go back to England for a while."

I was glad that Eddie understood, but I needed him. "I understand why you want to go back to England, but I need you here, mate; the most important part of our search has yet to be uncovered. Is there any chance of perhaps just cooling the relationship for a while?"

Eddie took a gulp of his drink. "Okay, I hear you; I will try and find the right moment to end it with her."

We walked back home in silence, the atmosphere feeling tense around us.

"Sorry, mate." I gave Eddie a bear-hug and a slap on the back, then watched him head back to his place.

When I got in, Olivia could sense my mood. "What's wrong?

Has something happened?"

I explained the difficult conversation me and Eddie had just had.

She was clearly upset. "Surely we can sort this out. Eddie thinks the world of her! I would even go as far as to say that I thought she was 'the one'."

I sighed. "Olivia, he knows what he needs to do: he has no choice but to dump Gianna."

Chapter 19

Without wishing to sound heartless, Eddie being single again brought benefits to the mission, as he threw himself into work.

We knew there was more to uncover – after all, we knew that this was the church used as the main treasury, and all contributions were brought here. There was no way that just an empty vault could be here.

For the next few weeks our time was occupied chiselling away at different parts of the crypt, to no avail. We were baffled.

One day, when Andreas and his team had left, me and Eddie found an unbroken part of the seat in the front pew to sit on, and hoped for some sort of divine intervention.

"The only area we have not disturbed is the altar; every other part of the church has been investigated."

We sat there, staring at the altar, which was cemented to the ground and tiled all around with ornate, discoloured tiles. This was the only area Father Luca had wanted protected.

"You do realize it's made of solid marble?" Eddie mused. "How the fuck do we move two tons of solid marble?"

I shrugged.

"Nathan, how long and wide would you say the crypt measures?"

"Ehm, if I was to hazard a guess, I'd say approximately six by six metres."

We sat there for a little longer, before the penny dropped. "I know what you're thinking," I grinned: "we drill a few metres from the altar, toward the hidden crypt, then go back down to see if this provides any clues."

Eddie nodded and replied: "What have we got to lose?"

We looked around at the tools the labourers had left behind, ready for the next day, and picked up the longest drill bit, which was a metre in length. Eddie attached it to the drill and, as I measured a few metres from the altar, toward the concealed crypt door, Eddie began drilling.

Eddie had drilled more than half the length of the drill bit, when the concrete flooring ended and he was drilling space. He stopped and nodded. "It's hollow beyond six-hundred millimetres."

We checked that the church door was closed, before going back down to the crypt, to see if we could see any signs of debris from where we had been drilling. "Eddie, leave the drill in place, to help us locate the area from below."

We measured the distance from the hole to the wall, went back down and started to drill.

Eureka! The wall softened.

We started to pull away at it, finally seeing a hollow compartment, through the ceiling of which our drill bit was plainly visible. Before long, we removed enough of the wall to make it clear that it had been added much later – to cover the Cardinal's sins?

Climbing through it, we walked single file, until we reached the area which I believed to be directly underneath the altar. The area opened out even as we approached, growing wider.

And there we could see dozens of rusted chests, stacked three high, side by side, the full width of the crypt. This was, no doubt in our minds, the place where Cardinal Bertocelli stored the donations from all over Italy.

To think of how we had felt when we uncovered the first hidden treasure, nobody could now envisage how we were feeling, knelt in front of this mountain of wealth. Both of us remained speechless for what seemed an eternity. Eddie broke the silence with just one word: "Priceless!"

Neither of us had ever encountered such a display of unique

jewels: an array of stones varying in both colour and size; so many gold and silver goblets; other ornate pieces the likes of which we had only ever seen in history books, and perhaps museums. There were coins, thousands upon thousands of them – unfortunately most of which would probably not be saleable.

"How does anybody put a value on this?" Eddie gasped.

I took a few pictures on my phone to show Olivia. For now, the treasure needed to remain in its place; we didn't need to attract any attention to ourselves. Using some ready-mix cement, we bricked up the entrances, concealing any trace that we had discovered any hidden areas.

Eddie went home to shower, before he would come back to mine and Olivia's.

As soon as I put the key in the door, Olivia called out: "Where have you been? I've tried phoning both of you several times! I've had Gianna on the phone, wanting to know why Eddie was avoiding her calls; Marco has called several times; and Marco's wife called, asking if he was with you!"

"Sorry, sweetheart, I should have called when we realized we were going to be delayed. Any chance of a bite to eat and I'll tell you all about it?" I gave her a hug, and watched as she walked into the kitchen, playfully shaking her head as if Eddie and I were naughty schoolboys.

Why was Gianna calling Eddie? I thought he'd broken up with her. I waited for Eddie to come over and, after a bite to eat, I asked him: "Mate, have you actually told Gianna that you're not seeing her, or have you just dumped her with no explanation?"

After a big sigh, Eddie explained: "I'm not good at break-ups… especially when I love the girl."

"I'm sorry, mate, but you know what she does for a living. I don't think you have a choice."

"You're right. I'll call her now."

A few minutes later, Eddie sheepishly came back and said: "Right, I'm going to head over to Gianna's place."

I gave Eddie a hug, knowing that this was not going to be easy for him.

Olivia heard him leave and came back in. "Where's Eddie gone? He didn't even say goodbye!"

I explained to Olivia that Eddie had just stopped seeing Gianna, without actually breaking up with her.

"Oh, no! But, he's going to see her now?"

"Yes. You know, Eddie has no other choice but to end their

relationship; it wouldn't be fair to continue putting her or himself at risk. He's going to end it tonight."

"Poor Gianna! I know she thinks a lot of Eddie."

"Poor Eddie! The feeling is mutual."

We spent the rest of the evening looking at the photos I had taken on my mobile, and bringing Olivia up to speed with what Eddie and I had uncovered. It was good to spend some quality time with Olivia; however, my mind kept drifting to Eddie.

Soon it was late, and Olivia was ready for bed. "I know you're worried about your friend, but nobody can take somebody else's pain away."

Olivia was right, so we headed to bed.

Eddie showed up bright and early the next day.

"You look terrible," I told him. "Have you had any sleep?"

No reply, just a false smile.

"Was it bad? You look done in, mate."

Eventually, he spoke: "I think I handled it well, but I miss her already, Nathan."

I made us a coffee and we sat talking, until the hustle and bustle of the piazza echoed its sounds through the window shutters, to join us in the living room. Eddie gave me the shorter version of how he had decided to end things with Gianna. He had made up some cock and bull story of unfinished business back in England and it was best, for now, that she wasn't dragged into it.

"This was going to be difficult enough without making it final; I had to leave an opening for me, in the hope of wooing her back one day."

"I understand, mate."

We spent the rest of the morning discussing the new addition to our stash, before my phone started to ring.

"Marco, hello. Sorry I didn't call you back last night. Everything okay?"

Marco was brought up to speed, and suggested that me and Eddie come over for a meeting. Olivia took the opportunity to go and do some shopping; we arranged for her to come over to Marco's when she was ready. Marco assured me that Olivia would be okay, and that someone was assigned to look after her.

When we arrived, Marco was on the veranda, drinking Antonella's homemade lemonade and arranging transportation for the caskets to be removed from San Biagio Church. He informed us of his plan, and asked us to meet him the next day, outside the church. We agreed that meeting at lunchtime, when the piazza was busy with people going about their everyday lives, was best.

Then, with business taken care of, we spent the rest of the afternoon enjoying the tapas-style nibbles and refreshing lemonade, which was accompanied by mandarin-flavoured vodka. It was good to sit back and watch my closest friends laughing and joking together.

At that moment a car pulled up and a woman stepped out.

"Wow! Olivia, what have you done?!"

"Don't you like it, darling?"

"I love it! You look stunning!"

Olivia had spent the day shopping and had surprisingly had her hair cut short. There are not many women who can look sexy whether their hair is long or short, but this dame certainly still looked hot!

Antonella poured Olivia a glass of her homemade lemonade and a generous shot of mandarin vodka, decorated with a slice of fresh lime and ice. We spent the rest of the afternoon slowly getting intoxicated with Antonella's version of a cocktail, with very enjoyable company. The children were making us laugh, with their impressions of various members of the family, and

Marco encouraged them to mimic Eddie and myself. This brought screams of laughter, as we both profusely denied sounding anything remotely similar to their take on us, with counterattacks from the women, who congratulated them on their talents.

I looked over at Eddie, who was smiling and making small-talk with Marco's son Stefano, but I knew this was a difficult time for him. I noticed him checking his phone quite a lot – and from his face it looked like Gianna had taken the hint, and was not chasing after him.

Eddie decided to walk the three miles back to Terranuova. Olivia and I stayed on a while longer, already knowing that our personal taxi driver was on hand to take us home. Neither of us was in any shape or form fit to drive.

I went for a stroll with Marco to discuss the next step.

"I have booked a skip to collect the chests and deliver them to one of my warehouses," he told me.

"Is it safe?" I asked.

"Of course it's safe; no one in this town would dare cross Marco Mazzi."

The next morning, Eddie and I met Marco at the crack of dawn, outside the church as planned. The skip was already delivered by the time we got there, giving us plenty of time to dismantle the hidden wall, bring up the caskets, camouflage them with debris and load them into the skip. Marco had thought of everything, and even gave Andreas and his team a paid day off, so our activities would not arouse suspicion. We formed a human chain to bring up the caskets and trunks; it felt a little strange throwing them into the skip as if they were rubbish.

When all of the items were secured in the skip, we had just enough time to re-cement the wall down in the crypt before joining Marco, who was standing by the skip, making polite chit-chat with some locals. The skip lay in full view, for all of Terranuova to see.

Me and Eddie got into Marco's car, and followed the lorry carrying the skip down to the warehouse. There, we helped to unload the rusty chests, before paying the guy a substantial amount to totally forget all knowledge of this job – and, of course, us. He shook Marco's hand and seemed more than happy to be of service to such an honourable man who, there was no doubt, was held in high esteem in Arezzo. Marco took this in his stride, but I was proud that we were related. Perhaps this was why I was enjoying this mission so much: because it was in my blood! Well, this seems a good place to clarify that I enjoyed *most* of the mission, but definitely not being party to murder.

Back at Marco's home, the three of us were sat enjoying an espresso, when Marco asked: "Why did they have to put up a false wall in the crypt? After all, nobody had access to the crypt anyway."

"My theory, Marco, is that the cardinal received word that his conspiracy was uncovered by the pope, and soldiers were on their way to arrest him if they found any damaging evidence. So, the cardinal built a wall to conceal his treasure, out of sight of the soldiers."

"Makes sense," agreed Eddie. "My clever cousin has cracked the puzzle."

We laughed, then walked over to my car, which was still at Marco's house from the night before. Bidding Marco ciao, with a hug and a pat on the back, we drove back home.

Over the next few weeks, Eddie took regular trips to Marco's warehouse, to price each item in each chest – apart from certain items of historical interest, which I put to one side; these pieces belonged to Italy, and somehow I wanted to make sure they remained with their rightful owner. Finally, the valuation process was completed, and Eddie handed me the breakdown of each item, along with the total valuation.

My jaw dropped. “Is the decimal point in the right place?”

“Yes, Nathan; I don’t make mistakes with money. The amount totals approximately – give or take a few thousand and depending on the market – four-million, six-hundred-and-three-thousand, eight-hundred pounds. And that’s not including the items you put in a separate container to give back to the people of Italy. Oh, and here’s some papers that were in the bottom of one of the trunks.” He handed me a leather pouch.

I was overwhelmed. As well as the monetary value of our find, there was also the acknowledgement that there was absolutely, no doubt in my mind, concrete evidence of a plot to overthrow the English Monarchy by a group of Catholics around Europe. This was a scary thought. I wondered why the plot did not succeed, and how the world would be now if it had.

Unlike the other documents, this one was in Greek. I took the leather case and its contents home to study.

I now needed to get my head around how we were going to arrange getting four-and-a-half-million pounds worth of jewels back to their rightful owners.

Eddie decided to go back to London for a break, and I agreed that this was a good idea. The next morning, I dropped him off at Pisa airport, and drove back home taking the scenic route.

I stopped in a café, wishing I had the answers to my next mission: finding a way to hand over a large proportion of the treasure without attracting any attention; I didn't want any of us to end up at the bottom of a lake, or with some other gruesome ending. How could we continue to pursue this thread of investigation without any major consequences? Eddie had already given up his relationship with Gianna for the mission; what would I end up losing if I continued? My mind was working overtime.

I wanted to bring closure to this project, but I also wanted answers to so many questions, including how Agostino really met his end. I owed this much to the man I loved as if he were my own father.

Finally, I was glad to be back in Terranuova.

"Hi, darling. Is Eddie on his way back to England?" Olivia called out.

"Yep, I dropped him off in plenty of time to make sure he didn't miss his flight. What have you been up to while I was gone?"

"Oh, this and that. While you were out, Gianna called to ask if I wanted to meet up with her for a catch-up. I said I would check with you first, in case you had made any plans for us, then ring back. I imagine she really just wants news of Eddie. I didn't say anything about him going back to England. What shall I do? I don't like lying to her."

"Stall her for now. Ring and say that I have booked a surprise getaway for us, and let it slip that Eddie has gone back to London indefinitely. Say that you'll call her when we get back, to arrange a catch-up – that should keep her curiosity at bay for a while."

"Are we really going away?"

"Yes, it seems that way."

"Where?"

"Antwerp. I suggest you start packing – and perhaps include some evening wear, too; I think we can afford to mix business with pleasure on this occasion."

Chapter 20

I wanted to call Fredrik, but it was ten o'clock at night; perhaps a little late. Still, I felt impulsive and wanted to catch him unaware, so I started dialling his number.

Although the receiver was quickly picked up, no one spoke. I broke the silence: "Fredrik, are you there? It's Nathan. Can you talk?"

With a sigh of relief, Fredrik replied: "Hello, my friend. Sorry for the pause; I am always careful when the phone rings so late. How are you? Have you more business for me?"

"Definitely, but this time I will only be bringing a sample of what is on offer, and photographs of other items I think will be of interest to you."

"I am intrigued. Will Eddie be accompanying you?"

I wanted my plans to remain a little vague. "Most probably; it all depends on his schedule. If not, I will bring another close friend of mine. Good to speak to you again, as always, Fredrik; we can talk better when we meet face to face."

"Before you hang up, do you want our friend Hendrik to join

us?"

"That would be a good idea. I will call you tomorrow to make final arrangements."

"I will look forward to it. 'Bye for now."

Olivia could not contain her excitement. Although she enjoyed the work she was doing for our "project", she wanted a little more of the action; this was her now in the front line and she was buzzing. Although it was great to see her enthusiasm, being a typical man – perhaps a little chauvinistic at times – I had always just wanted to protect her, by not involving her too directly. But I learned long ago that this lady wanted to be treated as an equal, so, with Eddie in London, it made sense to take Olivia with me to Antwerp.

I left the booking to Olivia, with the following instructions: the accommodation had to be a basic, no-frills three-star hotel for the first two nights, followed by the luxury of a prestigious, upper-class hotel for the next two nights. The budget hotel needed to be booked as close to Antwerp station as possible, and the second a few miles outside. Although we may as well combine business with pleasure, I thought the only way I would truly relax would be to leave Antwerp.

Olivia looked very pleased with herself, especially regarding the second part of our trip. She booked us into a five-star hotel with an indoor heated swimming pool, offering a variety of spa treatments and a beauty salon offering a pedicure and manicure service.

I too was looking forward to this part of our trip – far more than the first part – for obvious reasons. Eddie was my backup man, and without him I had to remain on red alert at all times. Marco offered to send Mario with us for security, but I felt we were only taking a token number of goods to show Fredrik, and this did not warrant the protection.

We arrived at our destination the following evening. Walking up to the desk, Olivia informed the desk clerk: "Reservations for Mr. and Mrs. Jones."

The clerk welcomed us, handing her the key pass for our room. When we were out of earshot of anyone, I smirked; "Mr. and Mrs. Jones?"

Olivia grinned back at me and answered: "I thought it went well with our operation; you know, different names, disguises, that kind of thing."

"I think you've been reading too many books, Mrs. Jones."

That evening, I made another call to Fredrik, to confirm a meeting for the next morning. He suggested a bar, half a kilometre away from the shop, which suited me down to the ground; I wasn't going to take any chances, and was pleased with the public bar he chose for our meeting.

Leaving Olivia to freshen up, I took the elevator down to reception, to book a table for our evening meal.

"Oh, I'm sorry, sir, we do not have a restaurant, only a snack bar."

"No problem." Though, to be honest, when I asked Olivia to book a basic hotel, I didn't think it wouldn't have a restaurant!

By the time I went back to our room, Olivia was sliding her feet into a pair of open-toe stilettos. She looked stunning, in a fitted aubergine dress, which she accessorized with a simple white-gold necklace and matching earrings. Everything about her was classy, and the best part was that she was completely unaware of it.

"You look stunning, Mrs. Jones. I hope you have worked up a healthy appetite. I asked the desk clerk if she could recommend a good local restaurant and she suggested a Turkish one, which is literally a stone's throw away. The owner is a guy called Moustafa; the clerk asked if we could mention that the hotel recommended his restaurant to us."

"Turkish it is, then. Shall we go, Mr. Jones?"

We strolled a few minutes down the road, and could soon see that the restaurant was already busy with diners – always a good sign.

The waiter greeted us as we entered, and asked if we cared to have a drink at the bar whilst we waited for a table; he estimated that the wait would be about twenty minutes. As promised, I relayed that the restaurant was recommended by the hotel, a message which the waiter quickly went to pass on to a man who looked very much like the manager or owner of the establishment. He seemed pleased by the recommendation, and came over to personally greet us.

"Good evening. I'm Moustafa. Welcome to my restaurant. I hope that you enjoy your evening with us."

We ordered two Bellinis and, making my excuses to go to the gents, I asked the waiter if it was possible to have a window seat. At that, I handed him a small box, containing a white gold ring decorated with white diamonds, asking if he could bring a bottle of his finest Champagne after we had eaten our main course, along with two flutes.

As we discussed the finer details, the waiter added to my ploy by asking: "Would you like me to decorate the lady's flute with a fine, red ribbon tied in a bow, so that she knows to look in the glass?"

"That's a brilliant idea! I like it."

I went back to the bar and waited for our allocated waiter to lead us to the table.

I knew that Olivia liked to sample various dishes, so for our starters we agreed on a platter called *"Pilaki for Two"*. Pilaki is a Turkish-style meze, containing several dishes cooked in an array of sauces, using onions, garlic, carrots, potatoes and tomato paste; the main herb; I've been told, is coriander. As we were going to have Champagne after our main meal, I suggested a light rosé wine to accompany our food.

The starter was more than generous, so we tried hard not to order heavy dishes for our main – but this was to prove difficult. Olivia ordered a dish called *incik*, which is lamb on the bone, cooked very slowly in the oven with green peppers and carrots, accompanied by potatoes in a tomato sauce. I ordered a dish called *izmir kofte*: a spicy minced sausage served with a mint yoghurt dip, served with a side dish of rice. The hotel clerk wasn't kidding when she said the food was very good; we were certainly not disappointed.

I was getting a little nervous as the evening progressed, knowing that there was the small matter of a proposal to come.

The waiter came over and asked if everything was to our satisfaction; we smiled and nodded, indicating that we were both pleased with our selection. Next was dessert. "Paklava with pistachio for two," I said, with a nod to the waiter.

Then, I took Olivia's hand and placed it between my palms. Looking her in the eyes, I whispered: "I love you, darling, and I am so glad you gave us a second chance." I kissed her hand.

Right on cue, the waiter brought over two Champagne glasses, giving Olivia the one tied with the red ribbon; he placed the bottle of Champagne in a silver bucket, filled with crushed ice.

When Olivia glanced into her glass, she noticed the sparking ring at the bottom; her mouth opened and she looked at me. As I stood up and got down on one knee, Olivia's face went a few shades redder; the tears in her eyes sparkled as much as the stones in her ring. I tipped the ring from the bottom of the glass and placed it on Olivia's engagement finger.

"Everybody is staring at us, Nathan," she whispered.

"I think they are waiting for your reply, Olivia. I already bought you a ring with your favourite black diamonds; that was for friendship. With this white diamond ring will you do me the honour of being my wife; my better half?"

There was a long pause, as she looked at me. The restaurant was silent; you could hear a pin drop.

"You do realize that I can't stand up until you give me an answer," I said, through clenched teeth.

"Yes, yes and yes!" she suddenly gushed. "I would be so proud to be Mrs. Doyle!"

I swept her in my arms and kissed her – to the sound of clapping and cheering from the entire restaurant.

We still managed to eat our dessert and enjoy the Champagne.

Then, Olivia said: "I have to make a call to Mum. Then I have to send a few texts to my close friends…" Olivia was still talking when she stepped outside to call her mum. It was a long-distance call; she lived in New Zealand, where she had emigrated to after meeting Olivia's stepfather.

I watched Olivia on the phone; her head swayed from side to side as she paced backward and forward, like an excited child. Apart from Eddie, there was nobody I had the urge to call; it felt inappropriate in the circumstances. I decided to leave it for another time.

After dinner, feeling truly intoxicated, as if on another planet, we headed back to our hotel room.

Chapter 21

The next morning, we drove to the Hilton Antwerp. There was no comparison to the hotel we had just left; in contrast, the Hilton Antwerp was oozing opulence, as one would expect of a hotel of this grade.

After checking us both in, under the name of Mr. and Mrs. Remy, I left Olivia to enjoy a day of pampering. I tried to make tracking us difficult by using different names, and went one step further, not checking out of the previous hotel, just in case we were followed.

I planned to meet Hendrik and Fredrik at the bar in the Radisson BLU Astrid Hotel. I arrived fifteen minutes earlier than my guests, wanting to make sure that I was not being followed. I ordered a latté coffee; I wanted my wits about me.

I watched as my two "buddies" arrived. After the customary greetings were exchanged, I ordered coffees and an assortment of biscuits for us, then proceeded to show them the few samples of the goods I had brought with me, as well as the photos of other items, which could be for sale if the price was right. I could see from their faces that they were impressed. And they were undoubtedly interested; no poker face could hide what they were thinking.

Hendrik kicked off the negotiations: “Not bad. I am sure I can find customers who, at a reasonable price, may be interested.”

I smirked at his blasé approach. Fredrik too gave him a scornful look, as if he too was wondering what his partner was playing at. He expressed his own stance on what was on offer.

“I think we all know that they are more than ‘not bad’, and that anybody interested in jewels would give their right hand to own them.”

Hendrik sheepishly accepted he was perhaps downplaying the objects, and reassured me that he was definitely interested in the gems. “Is everything in the photos for sale?”

I sat back and, taking a deep breath, responded: “It can be – at a realistic price for such rare items. I am looking for one buyer who will purchase the entire collection from me. I’m looking for a rock bottom price of…” I paused for a moment, keeping them in suspense as I looked them straight in the eyes, before continuing: “I’m looking for a total of two million… pounds sterling.”

You could have heard a pin drop.

After a bated breath, Fredrik broke the silence: "We are interested. However, we need to discuss how long it will take for us to shift such valuable items."

Hendrik asked for two months to round up his usual purchasers; I wanted to wrap up the deal within four weeks. With a lot of shaking heads and negotiating, we finally agreed to exchange money for goods in six weeks. I knew as well as they did that the jewels were worth much more, but I also knew that they were taking a risk selling such items. Two million would cover our expenses and the restoration of San Biagio Church; I was more than happy with the deal. We shook hands and agreed to make contact within four weeks, with the final arrangements.

I got up from the table first, wanting to make my exit as quickly as possible.

I took a taxi back to the first hotel, just to see if I was followed. There, I settled the bill, and was asked by the desk clerk if I would like her to order a taxi. I chose to decline, thinking it would be best to hail a taxi en route.

I asked the taxi to drop me off about a kilometre from the Hilton Antwerp, and walked the rest of the way. By the time I got to the hotel, I needed a bath and a well-earned nap.

Olivia was busy having the works done. She deserved it; she

was the woman that made my days worth getting up and my nights worth going to bed for.

I took a long soak in a bath which could easily fit two people, before crashing out on the king-size four-poster bed, drifting off before you could say: "1537 Conspiracy."

We were certainly going to make the most of the evening ahead, as we knew it was back to business first thing in the morning.

Ironically, the hotel had a dinner and dance on that night, and Olivia made full use of this by dressing up to the nines, asking that, just for tonight, we didn't mention the project, the family or anybody else, for that matter.

I held her hands, staring at the black diamond ring on her right hand and the white diamond ring on her left. "That is the least I can do: enjoy an evening with the person who means the most to me in this world." I kissed her on both hands, before starting to change into evening attire.

Then, linking arms, we took the elevator downstairs to the restaurant.

The atmosphere was perfect: good food, music we could actually dance to and company which couldn't be better. We ate, drank and danced the night away, before falling asleep in exhaustion.

The next day, after a hearty breakfast, we took a stroll around the town, looking like average tourists.

I arranged with the first hotel we stayed in to pay a premium and leave the Alfa for two extra nights, giving them a story about visiting friends who had no car parking facilities. We then found a quirky café in the square, where we sat to discuss what we needed to achieve before leaving.

"We have two million pounds worth of jewels to transport from Italy to Antwerp. We need a plan." I was starting to surprise myself; I was beginning to sound like a detective, thinking outside the box.

We needed to find a place where an exchange on this scale could take place. We hired a car for the day, and decided to leave the tourist area and drive down by the docks; this was where we came across a car park, overlooking the quay on the river side. I drove into the car park and, reading the information board, could see the benefits of doing the exchange here: the car park was open twenty-four hours and parking was free, which meant that on the day there would be no fluffing about for change, or estimating how long to put on a ticket, let alone nosey traffic wardens. There was also, very close, a road sign directing users to the motorway heading for Brussels. Bingo! This seemed the ideal meeting place.

Now for the hard part: how does one transport two million pounds of jewels in one trip, without suspicion? I had my work cut out.

The next morning, we picked up the Alfa and headed back to Italy, knowing we had only six weeks to set the whole plan in motion. It felt good to leave Antwerp, and I enjoyed the freedom of leaving any woes to one side.

Olivia, the road and me – what more could a man want? I laughed to myself when I recalled that I might have lost her forever, due to my commitment phobia; I was relieved that she had given me this second chance.

Chapter 22

It was good to be back in Terranuova.

Olivia put on the percolator for hot coffee and biscotti, while I unpacked the bags and opened the shutters and windows, to freshen up the place. It felt good to be home.

My thoughts drifted to Eddie, so I decided to give him a quick call. "Hi, mate. How's things?"

Eddie updated me with a "man's" version of events, and went on to ask if anyone had asked after him.

"No, mate, but when I went over to see Marco, Antonella mentioned that she saw Gianna in the square on a recent market day." He obviously wanted an update, so I told him that Antonella had gone on to say that Gianna looked pale and seemed to be putting on a brave face.

"Did Antonella say if she had asked after me?"

"No, mate. That doesn't mean anything, though; some of us are good at hiding our feelings, aren't we?" There was a pause before I continued: "Eddie, it's time for you to come back, mate. Are you okay with that?"

Another silence, then: "Yes, mate, when do you need me to come back?"

"Yesterday."

We laughed.

"Okay. Today is Tuesday; shall we say Thursday? I'll text you the details."

"Look forward to it, mate."

The next day I received a text from Eddie: *"Flight TOM5154, arriving Pisa on Thurs, 11.25am."*

That left me tonight to make a list of everything that needed to be covered before, during and after our trip back to Antwerp. It was important that we covered every detail, as I knew that it was not just mine and Olivia's futures at stake, but Eddie's, Marco's and that of his family.

Before long, my eyes were getting tired. I looked up and could see Olivia fast asleep on the sofa; glancing at the clock, I couldn't believe that it was one o'clock in the morning. Gently waking Olivia and guiding her to our bedroom I locked up and we turned in for the night. My mind tried desperately to switch off, but it seemed forever before I finally did.

In the morning, we popped over to Marco's.

I brought him up to speed with the plans, while the women sat on the veranda making small-talk. Me and Marco left the girls and went to his lockup, so that I could return the selected items taken over to Antwerp, for Hendrik and Fredrik to inspect.

We then dropped by San Biagio Church, for our planned meeting with Andreas. Marco had asked Andreas if he and his team could resume work again, which had been postponed until I came back, so that we could keep up the pretence of needing either Eddie or myself on site. We agreed times and dates and bade Andreas goodbye.

"Are you staying for dinner?" Antonella asked.

I looked over at Olivia and answered: "Thanks, Antonella, but can we pass tonight? I have a few things to do."

We kissed them goodbye and headed home.

That night, I again made notes for me and Eddie to cover when he returned.

Olivia woke me with a cup of tea.

I was shocked that I was still asleep at nine o'clock. I jumped up, took a gulp of tea, quickly washed and dressed and, with no time to spare, headed for the airport. Pisa airport was at least an hour and a half's drive away, and I couldn't believe that, of all days, my lack of sleepless nights had caught up with me today!

By the time I arrived at the airport, Eddie was already standing outside waiting for me. It was good to see him. After the usual greetings, I took his bag and we headed back to Terranuova. He looked a little thinner, but I restrained myself from saying so, as I didn't think he would appreciate it.

As we arrived in Terranuova, Eddie seemed quieter than usual. Still, with no need for conversation, we headed home and I parked the car.

Olivia texted me to say that she had just popped out to get some shopping, and to tell Eddie that she will be sure to bring back a packet of his favourite chocolate and caramel biscuits.

"I've arranged for us to meet up with Marco tonight, at eight o'clock."

Eddie looked at me, then surprised me by saying: "Give a man a break; I've only just got back."

With that, Eddie said that he would come over at about six o'clock, then headed straight across the piazza to his rented flat.

I was starting to get a little concerned, particularly as Olivia was still not back. I gave her a call.

"Hi, hun, where are you?"

"Hi, darling. Hope you don't mind, but Gianna called me and asked if I fancied a coffee. I didn't want to tell you in my text, as I knew Eddie would be with you."

"Is she okay?"

"I'll fill you in when I get home."

"Do you need a lift back?"

"No, it's okay; Gianna said she would bring me home."

"Well, there's no rush; me and Eddie are going over to Marco's for… a bite to eat."

"Okay, darling, see you later."

Eddie looked very smart.

"Wow, I'd fancy you myself if I was a girl!" I joked.

He smiled, then asked: "Are we waiting for Olivia?"

"Eh, no, she's making her way home as we speak." I didn't want to say that she was with Gianna, so I changed the subject straight away.

Then, picking up the keys and the list for tonight's meeting, we locked up and headed over to Marco's.

When we arrived, the children ran to greet us. I handed them a small jar of assorted sweets to share, which Olivia had bought when we were visiting Antwerp. Antonella welcomed us and pointed over to the conservatory, to signal that this was where Marco was.

"No Olivia?" she asked.

"No, not tonight. But she said to say hello."

On the table there was an array of tapas-style dishes, accompanied by side-plates for us to help ourselves and three glasses. There were two jugs, one containing sparkling water and the other Antonella's famous homemade lemonade, both jugs garnished with slices of lemon and cubes of ice.

Marco pointed to the jugs with a disappointed look; "I thought we all needed to keep clear heads tonight. We have a lot of… eh, how do you say… *integrate* business to discuss."

Eddie and I grinned, knowing that Marco had meant to say "intricate".

"You are right, Marco," I said: "we all need to have clear heads. Every detail is crucial for this transaction to be a success."

We then tossed ideas backward and forward, changing aspects of the plan as we debated and agreed on the best way to proceed.

We agreed to stick to the car park by the docks for the exchange, and mapped out the route back home.

We were discussing vehicles and ways to conceal such a quantity of jewels, when I took a break to call Olivia; I needed to know she was safely home.

"Hi, hun. Just wanted to check you were home."

"Safe and sound. You okay?"

"Yep, just thrashing out some stuff with Marco and Eddie; didn't want to mention it earlier, when you were with Gianna. Talking of which, how is she?"

"She's fine. I'll fill you in when you come home."

"Okay, hun, but it might be a late one, so you can update me in the morning. I'll try not to wake you. Sweet dreams. I love you."

"Ditto."

I walked back into the conservatory, where a much-needed double espresso and bite-sized pastries were waiting for me. We joked about how Marco remained slender, with such temptations surrounding him daily. With a mischievous look on his face, he answered: "Why do you think Italians have siestas, my friend?" We all laughed.

Then, after a welcome break, we got back to the job at hand.

With a pen ready to tick every point agreed, we summarized with a checklist: Marco would organize the transport; Aldo and Ernesto would take a Mercedes Sprinter van and share the driving between them; Marco, Eddie and I would ride together, in a 4x4 Mitsubishi.

With the transport sorted, our attention then turned back to the work Marco would need to carry out, in order to modify the vehicles, so that the jewels could be concealed. The engines would also need to be upgraded, to ensure a speedy escape, should it be necessary.

Chapter 23

Over the next few days, Olivia was preoccupied with translating the scripts.

"Are you okay? You seem puzzled," I asked.

"I'm fine; it's just that something about the connections mentioned in this document concerns me. The document dates back to 1534; it was written in Greek, from Sir Thomas More to Cardinal Bertocelli. So, according to this document, not only could Thomas More read Greek, but he knew about the conspiracy, and was writing to Cardinal Bertocelli to find out about the latest plans to invade England. I know you told me that Sir Thomas More did not take the oath to acknowledge that the king was the supreme head of the Church of England, so for this reason he would have been in danger of being arrested for treason, but how did Thomas More know about the conspiracy in the first place?"

I paused in thought, then replied: "I can only assume that Thomas More met the cardinal on one of his visits to the Vatican, and they shared the same political views."

There was a moment's silence before I continued: "Do you realize that this document will rewrite history? And there will be questions of why it was written in Greek."

Taking a gulp of coffee, Olivia said, "The latter part, Nathan, is simple: many scholars could not read, write or speak Greek, but many knew Latin, so by corresponding to each other in Greek, it meant that they were in the minority, and if intercepted the document's secrets would be more difficult to decipher."

"Makes sense. All I know is that at some point in the future we will have to release these documents to historians for the world to see. In the meantime, we will keep them secure, until they are handed over. I think I need a drop of Grappa in my coffee to absorb all this information!"

Olivia joined me in a medicinal drop of the hard stuff, and we tried to digest the sequence of events as they had unfolded. I decided to call Eddie, for any updates at his end, and to go over the plans.

"Hi, Eddie, how's it going? Are you still at the church with Andreas?"

"Yes. The good news is that in a couple of days the church will be finished, and ready to hand back to Father Luca," Eddie responded.

"That is good news, Eddie. Can you get back as soon as you can?"

"Why, what's up?" Eddie asked.

"Just business, mate. Explain when I see you."

The building work at San Biagio Church had now reached the stage where it was okay for Andreas and his men to be left unsupervised by myself or Eddie. I was surprised to see Eddie back so quickly; less than ten minutes.

"I was not expecting you back so soon."

"There wasn't much for me to do at the church, and as there's now no danger of them uncovering anything we don't want them to, I was just a spare part. Andreas has the phase under control."

"Good. I've got some news for you: the documents we found in the silver box were written in Greek, between Cardinal Bertocelli and our very own Sir Thomas More, proving that they were conspiring together! Do you know who I'm talking about?"

"Yes, I've heard of him, but I don't know his life story."

So, Olivia proceeded to tell Eddie all about our Sir Thomas More, and what the documents had unveiled. When Olivia had finished explaining it all to Eddie, it was obvious that he had a lightbulb moment. Realizing the importance of what we had uncovered, he said:

"It's hard to believe that we have discovered such important documents. Now I understand why it's so important that we keep them safe for the future."

"Eddie, just one more thing: I want you to phone Hendrik to confirm the details of the exchange. Make sure he repeats the time, the place and the day back to you."

"Actually, he's already called me. He just wanted to confirm that he had taken down all the details correctly, and that it was still at the Riverside Quay car park. I confirmed, so there is no need for another call."

"Good. I'm going to call Marco to arrange us going over to see him, and ask if Ernesto and Aldo can also be there, as I'm thinking of adding some changes to our plan."

"What are you up to?" Eddie asked.

"Just in case Hendrik has ideas of his own, I thought it would be best if we had a backup plan, in which we drive into Luxembourg and make the exchange there, instead. I have done some research and found a hotel called Sofitel Europa; it has an underground car park, just before the entrance. We arrive the day before the exchange, phone Hendrik and tell him that the car has broken down, and ask can we meet in Luxembourg Sofitel Hotel's underground car park, instead."

"What if he says no?"

"There is no reason why he should say, unless he was planning something of his own. So, shall we go ahead and let Marco and the rest know of our updated plans?"

Eddie nodded and added: "Actually, Nathan, I agree with you; we don't want to take any chances."

I made the call. "Hi, Marco. Any chance of coming over for a short meeting, with you and the boys?"

"Of course. Shall we say in about twenty minutes?"

"See you soon, Marco."

I gave Olivia a call, to let her know where Eddie and I were going. "Hello, darling. Where are you?"

"Ciao! I'm just doing some retail therapy."

"Enjoy. I'm just ringing to let you know that I'm heading over to Marco's with Eddie. Should be back early evening."

"Okay, darling; see you later. Do you want me to prepare dinner?"

"How about we go out tonight?"

"Sounds good. See you later."

As we arrived, Marco was standing outside his car showroom,

chatting up two attractive women.

"Hello Nathan, Eddie, let me introduce you to my friends Juliana and Maria."

We made polite introductions, with Marco explaining that I was his cousin, and Eddie my friend from England. Marco went on to say that the girls were the best dressmakers in Italy, so if we ever needed any clothing altered they were the girls to get in touch with. We nodded dutifully.

After saying goodbye to Marco's friends, he led us to his office, asking Ernesto and Aldo to close up shop and join us. We made coffee and got straight to business.

Everyone was in agreement regarding the backup plan.

"I have already checked out the location, and it is ideal for motorway links, just in case anything does go wrong," I explained. "Eddie, can you hand everyone a copy of the new location, with detailed plans including times, dates and maps?"

We were as ready as we could be, so after some chit-chat we got up to head back home.

Before parting, I changed the subject to a more upbeat one: "By the way, are you aware that the church is ready to be handed back to Father Luca this coming Thursday?"

Marco replied, with a beaming smile: "Yes I am. Don't

worry, Nathan; everything is under control."

"So, are you happy with a little ceremony to hand the keys back to Father Luca, and lead the speeches?"

"Yes. In fact, don't laugh, but I have already prepared my speech, and roped Antonella to make one, too. I have invited all the locals and the council officials."

"Perfect, Marco. Well done."

On the way back to town, we dropped in to see Andreas and his men, who were still busy, working as hard as ever on the final touches to the church. As I was not going to be making a speech, I wanted to thank Andreas and his team personally for the brilliant job they had done, bringing the local church back to all its glory.

"Will you all be coming to the celebration on Thursday?"

In unity, they all replied: "Sì, non ci mancherebbe per il mondo *(Yes, we wouldn't miss it for the world)*!"

The big day arrived.

Me and Eddie were up early, as we were due to meet the florist and various other representatives of local establishments. It was a little after eight-thirty in the morning, and already there were people waiting to get into the church, to carry out their various tasks. After we'd greeted everyone, they followed us in and began transforming the church, ready for the celebrations. Garlands of flowers were draped at the end of each pew, and large displays of flower arrangements were put together, as if by magic. A table was decorated at the front of the church, with glasses and bottles of Champagne for the guests, and another table was covered with woven baskets, filled with individually wrapped slices of local panettone.

I felt a sense of achievement uncovering the secrets and history of Cardinal Bertocelli, and a sense of sadness that it had come at the cost of my old friend Agostino's life.

Back home, Olivia was getting ready, and after a quick coffee I jumped into the shower. This was followed by holding up a variety of shirts and suits, to decide which would best serve in the hot Italian weather. I settled for a grey suit.

I watched through the sitting room window, as Eddie strolled across the street in a cream suit with a pink shirt. I whistled at him before he rang the doorbell, making him look up toward the window. "Very dapper, Signor Eddie!" I went down to greet him.

Olivia joined us, looking stunning as always; she had chosen a pale-blue cotton dress for the occasion. I looked over in her direction and just stared at her for a while.

We arrived at the church just before midday, where there was already a small crowd of locals chatting, laughing and looking typically Italian, with animated hands contributing to every conversation.

By midday, Father Luca arrived, accompanied by council officials. They were soon followed in by Andreas, his merry men and their families. Marco, Antonella and their children came next, along with Alberto, who had really started the whole adventure, with just one phone call. After a lot of handshaking, everyone stood around the church building to listen to the speeches, hoping to discover who had gifted the money to carry out the repairs.

Father Luca was the first to make a speech. He thanked everyone for coming, and began to tell of the day that three very special people came to him, wanting to know why this beautiful church had not been restored to its original splendour; how they could not understand why the church was closed and left to stand empty, in ruin. He continued to explain that the reason for this had been not having the money to pay for the restorations needed. He then went on to say that, a few days later, these very generous people came back to see him, wanting to make a donation to the church. With teary eyes, he explained: "I thought the donation would be fifty or sixty euros. Never in my wildest dreams did I think that they were talking about fully restoring the church, so that it could once more open for all to come together and worship. The exterior of the church just looks fantastic now; I cannot wait to see what has been accomplished inside! May God be with you all – especially our anonymous benefactors; thank you. I would also like to thank Marco and his family for their help, and all the builders who have worked so hard on this project; thank you. I will now pass you over to Antonella."

Antonella stepped up. "When Father Luca told me about this story – that complete strangers had offered to donate all this money needed to restore our church – I just could not believe it. Our town has been given a special blessing by these angels, to get back what is the heart of our village. I am so proud to be married to my husband Marco, who organized the builders and managed regular meetings, to ensure that the project ran as smoothly as possible." Antonella's speech was momentarily interrupted by claps and nods. She continued:

"In just under six months, San Biagio has been restored, and is now ready to be handed back to Father Luca and the people of

Terranuova.

"Father Luca has given me a note written by one of our anonymous donors; it reads as follows:

"'*I walked into the church and saw a ray of light beaming on the altar, and a voice telling me that me and my friends have been chosen to reopen the doors to this dilapidated church. It is our pleasure that we can restore San Biagio for the people of Terranuova.*'"

Olivia put her hand over her mouth and gave a small cough, whilst Eddie could not even look at me, for fear of bursting into laughter.

The speeches continued from members of the council, before Marco was called forward to hand over the keys to the church.

As Father Luca turned around to put the key in the door, everyone started clapping and cheering. He opened the massive, dark wooden doors and, once again, the sunshine paved the way into the church.

As everyone was heading into the church, Olivia and Eddie looked at me in disbelief. "So, you had a calling from above to restore the church?" she teased.

"I just thought it sounded good."

"Come on, Angel Gabriel, let's go get a glass of bubbly... for medicinal purposes, of course."

The Champagne was flowing, and everybody was chatting and admiring the restored building. They were absorbing everything from the new plasterwork to the cleaned and fixed marble and the newly painted walls. The upholstery and artwork were brought back to life, the latter back hanging on the walls. The locals were clearly enjoying mingling once again in their local church. Once the celebrations were finished, Father Luca held Mass.

After prayers for the people of the town, loved ones and for the world generally, a few family members and friends started making their way back to Marco and Antonella's home, for a light lunch. Olivia and I stayed behind to help clean up, washing glasses and disposing of empty bottles of Champagne.

Finally, when boxes were packed and hired hospitality items handed back, we made our farewells to Father Luca, and left him to admire his beautiful church.

By the time we arrived at Marco's house, the food was already laid out on mismatched garden tables. There was a vast choice of antipasto, salad, cheeses, homemade pasta dishes and an assortment of cakes.

The celebration continued into the early hours of the morning, ending with most of us intoxicated, and not just on the alcohol, but the sequence of events leading to this historic day. There was a moment when Marco, Ernesto, Aldo, Eddie and me looked at each other and raised our glasses, knowing that this was just the beginning of what lay ahead.

"Hi, sleepyhead. I've made coffee."

I looked at Olivia standing over me, and reached for the clock to see what time it was. "Wow, it can't be eleven o'clock!"

"Well, that's what happens when you don't go to bed 'til two in the morning."

We chatted a little about the events of yesterday, and decided to make today a day of relaxing, just the two of us. I finished drinking my coffee and jumped into the shower, to get ready for a drive out of town with Olivia. I was just finishing getting dressed when the phone rang.

"Darling, it's Marco," Olivia said, handing me the phone. It suddenly dawned on me that our meeting in Luxembourg was only a few days away.

"Hi, Nathan, can you and Eddie come over to the warehouse this afternoon?" he asked.

"Is everything alright?"

"Yes, I just need us all to meet as soon as possible, that's all."

"Okay, we'll be there at two o'clock."

I knew that Olivia was going to be disappointed; we hadn't managed to spend any quality time together for a while. "I'm sorry, darling; Marco wants the boys to meet up and go over the plans. I will make it up to you – I promise."

She looked disappointed, but just said: "I'll hold you to that." She added that she would use the time to continue deciphering the remaining document.

I rang Eddie and asked him to come over.

At two o'clock on the dot we arrived at the warehouse.

Aldo waved us over to the side entrance and asked us to drive in, so that he could close the roller shutters. Standing at the back was Marco, looking very smug. "How do you like the transport I've arranged for us?"

We looked over in the direction Marco was pointing, and could see three very expensive looking cars. Eddie and I gave the cars a good looking over, as if buying them for ourselves.

With a big smile on his face, Marco added: "Well, have I done well or have I done well?"

Eddie just nodded, and I seconded it. "We're certainly driving to Luxembourg in style. But why three cars?"

"We need a backup, just in case one of the cars breaks down; one person in each car. As the jewels and firearms will be in the van, we will have two men in that."

"Whoa, hang on a minute!" Eddie said, looking concerned. "Nobody mentioned firearms!"

Marco frowned. "Guys, we're talking about millions of euros being exchanged! We have to be prepared; anything can happen. I wouldn't be surprised if they turn up fully loaded. We can't afford *not* to be carrying protection!"

Ruefully, we all nodded our agreement.

There was a short silence, before Marco continued to go over the final plans: "We leave here on Monday at four a.m.; Aldo will drive the van, with Ernesto as his passenger and his second pair of eyes, and us three driving the three cars."

Everyone then starting chipping in with *what ifs* and *how abouts*.

Once all avenues were exhausted, we drank coffee before heading home.

Olivia was sitting cross-legged on the floor, surrounded by papers, when Eddie and I walked in.

"Hi, gorgeous. You look busy."

"Well, if you two would like to make yourselves comfortable, I will tell you a little more about our documents. As stated before, this document is dated 1534. It begins as follows:

"*'Dumas, be patient. A ship has set sail from Geneo, with one hundred and fifty men-at-arms, and will be with you within twenty days of me writing this letter to you. Ten miles west of Plymouth my agent will contact you as soon as it is possible for him to do so, and escort you to the allotted meeting place. The ship is in the command of my dear friend Vinciano De Pisa, whom I trust implicitly.'*

"That's as much as I am able to translate, as this letter was not finished; perhaps it was only a draft – which leaves more questions for us: did the letter ever get finished? Did the finished letter ever get delivered?"

I attempted to answer Olivia's questions: "I don't know. All I know is that Sir Thomas More *was* executed—"

"Well, wait a minute... *was* he? Because, according to these, it seems that our friend Cardinal Bertocelli was attempting to rescue Thomas out of England by sea."

"Interesting."

Chapter 24

The day had arrived to put our plans into action; Luxembourg was beckoning.

All the alarm clocks in the house were set, but to my surprise Olivia was up before even the first went off, preparing coffee and croissants.

"Thanks, darling. Have you slept at all?" I asked, giving her a kiss on the neck.

"Not much," she replied, adding; "Nathan, I'm not going to lie, I'll be worrying until you are back safe and well."

Just as I was about to reassure her that no harm would come to me, the doorbell rang. I let Eddie in and explained to him that Olivia was feeling anxious about our trip, so be careful what he said; I didn't want to add to her concerns.

Eddie gave her a kiss on the cheek and, grabbing a warm croissant, tried to lighten the mood, by saying: "Just think, you'll have plenty of time to make plans for the future, and where you want him to take you for a well-earned shopping spree."

When Olivia didn't acknowledge what Eddie had said, after a

short pause he reassuringly added: "You just enjoy some time away from him. I give you my word I'll stick to him like glue; nothing's going to happen."

Olivia smiled and gave us both a hug.

We sat making idle chat, while we finished our coffee and snacks. Before long it was time to set off, to meet Marco and the rest of the gang at the warehouse.

It didn't look like anybody had got much sleep. We all arrived at the warehouse at pretty much the same time, and at least fifteen minutes earlier than planned; it was still dark and most of Arezzo was still asleep.

We were on the motorway by 4.15, heading toward Genoa, which was about 300km away. We drove without stopping. This was no hardship, because the drive was breathtaking, with only a handful of other vehicles on the road; the scenery was absolutely magnificent, and the road purposely erected on stilts, twisting through the valleys, made the drive a pleasure.

After five hours of driving, we eventually arrived in Genoa, stopped at the first services for a long, much-needed break. We were on schedule to arrive on time at our next stop Turin, which was about two hours away. After a good hour-long break, all fed and refreshed, we hit the road again, following the route to Alessandria, which would take us onward to Turin. We kept in single file, within the speed limit and enjoying the ride.

We soon reached the outskirts of Turin and, avoiding the centre, we took the ring road bypassing the city. We needed to make our last stop before crossing the Fréjus Tunnel, so we stopped at the next services to fill up with fuel, coffee and snacks. We sat at a large table outside the restaurant as, with map and pencil in hand, Marco informed us of the next stage of our journey.

"The next time we stop will be after crossing the Fréjus Tunnel, so it's best to buy drinks and snacks from here."

"How far will that be?" Eddie asked.

Marco continued: "The next stop is Metz, which will be about three-hundred kilometres away, and only twenty kilometres from our destination in Luxembourg.

So, with only a twenty-minute break, we purchased our supplies and were soon back on the road, making our exit for the Fréjus Tunnel and into France.

The drive was uphill all the way through the Italian Alps, the peak of the mountains still showered with snow, and bright blue skies reaching the summit and entrance to the tunnel. After that, it was all downhill, until gradually the mountains disappeared into the distance.

We reached Metz just before nightfall, came off the motorway and headed for the services. It was good to stretch our legs, get a bite to eat and grab a cup of coffee.

Then, with our needs met, we headed back to the cars, where Marco gathered us together, to finalize the last leg of the journey.

"As Nathan has already taken this route, we follow him. But if for some reason any of us lose sight of him, just head for the Sofitel Hotel and we will find you. Take the side turning, which is just before the entrance of the hotel, into the car park. This is where we will unload all the suitcases from the van – obviously as discreetly as possible. Nathan already checked for cameras on his last visit, so we know we will not be captured on C.C.T.V. until we reach the hotel entrance. There is a walkway directly into the hotel from the car park, so this is the route we will use. Aldo will take the suitcase with the weapons, and the rest of us will take the suitcases with the merchandise. We have booked three rooms separately, and we need to avoid being seen together as much as possible. For this reason, we'll check into the hotel at half-hour intervals and meet up two hours later, in the car park."

So, with everyone briefed, we headed for the last stretch of our journey.

*

As soon as we got to the hotel car park, Eddie contacted Hendrik as planned, to let him know that we needed to change our plan.

"Hello, Hendrik, it's your friend, Eddie. I'm sorry, mate, the car has broken down and we are stuck in Luxembourg."

Eddie was clearly interrupted by Hendrik, then continued to tell him: "No, Hendrik, Nathan doesn't want to hire a car. Hang on, I'll pass you to Nathan."

"Hi, Hendrik, I wish we could hire a car, but we have to stay here until the mechanic comes to sort out the car. Hendrik, I think this could be the perfect place for the exchange: it's nice and quiet; I've checked and there are no cameras; it's perfect." There was a short pause, as I gave him time to digest the new information.

"Okay, Nathan, where is this perfect place?"

With a thumbs-up, I continued my discussion with Hendrik. "Because the roads are so busy around this area, the car has been recovered to an underground car park opposite the Sofitel Europa Hotel, which is in the main district of Luxembourg."

"Okay, Nathan, we will see you tomorrow at the same time, in the underground car park."

Eddie and I headed up to our rooms, and I rang Marco to find out where he was.

"I'm in room 110; the others are already here. Give four knocks so I know it's you."

Heading to Marco's room, I updated the team with the good news.

"Bravo, Nathan. So far so good. Hendrik has taken the bait and it's all on for tomorrow morning."

Aldo opened a suitcase and handed each of us a semi-automatic pistol, with two extra magazines, fully loaded with ammunition. Eddie commented that he had never needed one of these in all of his years trading in Camden Town Market; we all laughed.

We decided to eat out and, heading out of the hotel individually, we met up in the car park, before heading to a bar about fifteen minutes' walk from the hotel.

That night, I struggled to get any sleep at all. Glancing in Eddie's direction, I could tell that neither did he. My mind was a whirl of thoughts.

I understood the precautions we needed to take, considering the amount of money involved in this exchange, but I wondered if we should have taken this road at all. I wondered where my life would have led me, if I never found the treasure in the first place: a normal life, a wife, kids, a house and endless bills, no doubt. On the other hand, maybe this was my opportunity to make a difference to people, while at the same time uncovering the truth about a part of history.

After a cold shower, we dressed. I put the handgun Aldo had given me down the back of my trousers, and Eddie did the same with his weapon. Then, we shook hands in silence and made our way to the lift, selecting the button for the reception area, before using the corridor which led to the entrance of the basement car park, where Marco and Aldo were already waiting for us.

"Where's Ernesto?" I asked.

"Ernesto is taking care of any cameras," Marco explained; "we don't want to leave any trace of us ever being here. We have one hour before Hendrik arrives, so me and Aldo will use the time to position two of the cars in the ideal spots, so that we can see you and Eddie at all times."

The cars were spaced to cover mine and Eddie's vehicle from every angle; as planned, the others would sit in their cars and wait.

Marco reiterated the order of events: "After the exchange, we let Hendrik drive out first, followed by Nathan and Eddie, and we will follow. Any questions?"

We all shook our heads and proceeded to put our plan into action. When we were satisfied that all precautions were taken, we all took our seats in the vehicles, ready for our arrivals.

After a very long twenty minutes, we saw a black 4x4 drive past us, with its lights blazing, and park up on the mezzanine level. The driver switched the headlights off, got out and walked toward the exit. A few minutes later, another car drove into the car park, parking in close proximity to the 4x4; once again, someone got out and walked toward the exit. I glanced at my watch: it was exactly four a.m. – the time we had arranged to meet Hendrik.

Five minutes passed, then ten, before another car entered the car park. As it drew closer, I could see that inside were Hendrik and Fredrik. I flashed my headlights, and it pulled into the parking space directly opposite us. Simultaneously, they both got out of the car.

Eddie and I mirrored them and started walking toward them. We shook hands.

Rather than the usual chit-chat, Hendrik observantly asked: "Is that a hired car or your own?"

"It's my car. A mechanic came out; fortunately for me he was able to repair the problem in about ten minutes: an electrical wire which had come loose."

The old boy seemed to accept my explanation, and proceeded to open the back of the car, to bring out two suitcases.

Eddie checked the contents, flicking through the bundles of money, before giving a nod that all was okay.

I walked over and opened the boot of my car, and brought out our two suitcases; this time, it was Hendrik's turn to check out the merchandise. He drew out a drinking vessel, made of pure gold laced in precious stones, and carefully studied it through his magnifying glass, verifying the authenticity of the diamonds. With excitement and a nervous twitch, he eagerly said: "Yes, magnificent! Let's continue with our exchange." So far so good.

But, just as we were saying our goodbyes, a shockwave blasted and echoed around our ears. Then another, and another… *bang, bang, bang!* Eddie and I hit the floor and tried to work out where the shots were coming from.

All I could see were two men, their faces covered by balaclavas, shooting at us. I raised my gun and fired back, then all hell let loose! It was a terrifying attack, with bullets ricocheting off the walls in every direction.

Marco and Aldo were running around frantically, taking cover and shooting back. The roar of automatic guns blasting was deafening, the haze of gun smoke blinding.

I saw two men go down, followed by a screeching sound of car tyres, as a vehicle made its quick exit through the car park. Marco was shouting: "Let's go! Let's go, Eddie! Get in the car."

I ran over to Hendrik, who was lying on the floor, shaking. With a tremor in his voice, he looked me straight in the eyes and said: "You have double-crossed me!"

"No, Hendrik, you fucking double-crossed me!"

I turned to the right of me, and could see that Fredrik was also in a state of shock. Meanwhile, Eddie was shouting at me to get the fuck in the car.

With full throttle, car tyres smoking, we made our escape out of the car park, toward the motorway and out of Luxembourg.

As we slowly calmed down, I saw that there was blood on the steering wheel. That was when I realized that Eddie had been hit.

Eddie saw me looking, and without my having to say a word, still driving like a bat out of hell, he said: "Don't worry; I'm alright."

It was too risky yet to take over the driving, so I instructed Eddie to continue to the nearest services, which were just outside of Metz.

Once there, I called Marco to see where he was, and was relieved to hear that he was only about twenty minutes away from us. I made Eddie comfortable and we waited for Marco, Aldo and Ernesto.

As soon as Marco's car pulled in, Aldo brought out a first-aid kit to attend to Eddie's wound. He had been hit by a bullet, a few inches below his chest, on the left-hand side, which fortunately missed his ribcage and inflicted only a flesh wound; that was good news. However, the wound was deep and needed substantial continuous pressure, to stop Eddie from losing too much blood.

Aldo looked at Eddie and, in his broken English, said: "You're not going to die, my friend."

With a smile on his face, Eddie replied: "Well, that's fucking good news, mate." With a nod, Aldo continued bandaging his wound.

We regrouped and unanimously agreed that time was paramount, making the decision that there would be no more stopping until we crossed the border into Italy.

Chapter 25

We drove in silence on the motorway, deep in thought about the chain of events. We drove through France and into Italy, stopping in Turin, by which time everyone was bursting for the loo, followed by coffee and a bite to eat. Nobody seemed interested in sharing their thoughts, but it was obvious we were all trying to work out what the hell had gone wrong. I was sure that if any of us had the answers we would have spoken. After filling up the cars with petrol we continued our six-hour journey back to the warehouse in Terranuova. No small-talk took place as we whizzed by the breathtaking scenery.

My mind was still trying to process the scene in the car park, from the terror of the gunshots still ringing in my ears, to the screeching of tyres, and the two unknown shooters. Who had double-crossed us? And were they dead?

It was late in the evening when we arrived back at the warehouse.

Marco had already arranged for a doctor to meet us there, to take care of Eddie's wound, and there were four wise men standing by, looking like bouncers at a seedy nightclub.

"Who the fuck are they?" I asked Marco.

"Don't worry, Nathan; they are bodyguards," Marco replied.

I shook my head, wondering if I was dreaming or fully awake. Marco went on to say that he didn't trust anybody now, and that was why he hired these guys. I guessed he was right; there were guys at the drop trying to kill us! These guys had made sure we got back safe. "Good thinking, Marco. We will solve this; no one will get away with betraying us."

The doctor was kept busy; after stitching Eddie up, he attended to Ernesto, who had been shot in the leg. The bullet had gone straight through, and he was badly in need of stitches of his own.

"Don't worry about Ernesto," Marco told me; "he has been through worse than this." Marco went on to take stock of the situation, telling me to go home. "We will talk tomorrow, Nathan, when we have all rested. One last thing: don't let Olivia know about any of this; the less she knows the better, capiche? If she asks about Eddie, tell her he is staying here for the evening."

I nodded in agreement, bade everyone goodnight and was opening the car door to leave, when Eddie called out: "Before you go, I have a surprise for you all. Open the boot of the car,

Nathan."

I did as Eddie asked, and to my surprise there sat four suitcases. I clicked open the cases, one by one; sure enough, there was the money in two, and the jewels in the others.

"How the fuck did you do end up with the lot?! Don't tell me that's how you ended up getting shot!"

Eddie had a grin sprawled right across his face. "Yep, that's how I ended up getting shot. So, from now on you can call me Eddie the Kid!" We laughed, patted one another on the shoulders and called it a night.

One of the bodyguards escorted me home, waiting until I had shut the front door before driving away.

Olivia was waiting for me and, after giving me a warm, emotional welcome back, immediately wanted to know how it all went, followed by where Eddie was. She told me how hard it had been for her not to keep calling, to see if we were alright. I explained that Eddie was staying over with Marco for the night, as he was not feeling very well. I added that, selfishly, I agreed it was for the best, because I didn't want Eddie to come back with me; I wanted the evening to be about us. I was relieved when this satisfied her.

With a smile that said a million words, Olivia opened a bottle of wine and we sat back on the settee enjoying some light antipasti dishes, with Lionel Richie in the background. It was good to be home...

*

The next morning, we all met up at the warehouse.

Marco poured everyone a coffee from the espresso machine, and we all sat around the table in his office trying to figure out what exactly had happened. Marco gave us news regarding the two strangers in the car park; according to the local news in Luxembourg, the men were not dead but badly wounded. The police said it was a gangland shooting; perhaps a drug deal which had gone terribly wrong. He informed us that he had phoned several of his contacts to find out if there was anyone that would be capable of pulling this off, but to no avail. We went backward and forward with questions, trying to find answers.

Finally, with pen poised, I asked: "Who knew about the exchange? Because Hendrik, whilst lying on the floor, terrified, accused *me* of double-crossing *him*!" I looked around the room angrily and continued: "Who the fuck knew about our plans, because it didn't seem to me that it was Hendrik who betrayed us?!"

We all started looking at each other.

Days and nights went by and still no answers, so I took matters into my own hands. I decided to go to Antwerp, to pay a visit to Hendrik.

I called Eddie, to let him know I had booked us a flight back to Antwerp.

"Are you fucking mad?!"

"I don't think so. If something doesn't make sense then it can't be right. I need to know who's responsible for this – because I don't think it was Hendrik."

Having taken an early flight the next morning, we arrived in Antwerp at nine o'clock.

We took a taxi to the city centre, and walked from there to Fredrik's jewellery shop. The door was locked, so I rang the bell.

Fredrik opened the door. "I never thought I would see you again," he said.

I wanted to see Hendrik. "Where's Hendrik? I need to talk to him."

As calm as a cucumber, Fredrik responded, "That would be

very difficult, my friend: he's dead."

"What?!"

Fredrik explained that, on that fateful morning, he had managed to get Hendrik back into the car and make an exit before the police arrived. Fredrik continued how Hendrik had then fallen forward in his seat; he realized immediately that his friend was having a heart attack. "I rushed him to the hospital, where he passed away later that day.

"I have lost a very dear friend. He may have not been an easy man to understand – he was a man with a vast amount of wealth, who collected precious objects not for their monetary value, but because he liked them – but he was a gentle and kind person, and I will miss him immensely."

Both Eddie and I conveyed our condolences at the awful news – and our apologies at how things had gone.

Once he recomposed, I looked at Fredrik and asked: "So, I assume you would be very interested to find out who betrayed us and bring them to account?"

Without any hesitation, Fredrik replied: "Yes, I would; he was my best friend. His last words to me, as I held his dying hand, were: 'I had nothing to do with the incident in the car park'. I never doubted it."

We sat with the old boy a little longer, until we felt it was the right time to bid Fredrik goodbye.

"Before we go, can I ask if there has been anything in the last few months which seemed a little suspicious to you – you know, a bit odd? Did Hendrik ever mention any of his investors?"

"No, I don't think so," Fredrik replied.

"If you think of anything, however small, can you call me? I give you my word that I will do all that I can to get justice for your friend."

"Thank you."

We left the shop, both a little affected by the kind words Fredrik had attributed to his best friend, which had made us even more determined to find out who was responsible.

We arrived back home late that evening.

Olivia looked surprised to see us. "I wasn't expecting to see you 'til tomorrow?" she expressed, startled.

"There was no point in staying. Our purpose was to gain information, but all we learned was bad news regarding Hendrik. I'm afraid he died later that evening, in hospital."

"Poor man! How did he die?"

I looked at Eddie, suddenly remembering that Olivia knew nothing about the shooting. Calmly, I replied: “He died of a heart attack.”

There followed a small silence, before Olivia suggested that we drink a toast to the poor man that evening.

“That’s a very good idea, Olivia.”

The following day, I rang Marco and told him all about the meeting Eddie and I’d had with Fredrik.

Although Marco was sad to hear that a man had died, he was concerned that this did not leave us any closer to finding out who was responsible for the double-cross.

“Marco, I think we should bide our time. These rats will know by now that we have both the jewels and the money. Let’s entice them out of their hiding place. I’ve had time to think about this, Marco, and I think that if we all go back to our normal working patterns – you know, business as usual, without bodyguards – we will draw the culprits out. We must be prepared to do whatever is necessary to solve this, because I’m not prepared to keep looking over my shoulder for the rest of my life!”

Marco hesitantly agreed.

The next few weeks were very uneventful. We all kept in touch daily, and nobody reported any suspicious activities. Everyone involved with the selling of the jewels was paid, and the rest of the money and jewels were safely hidden, until the time was deemed safe to decide where we go from here.

Just as I thought the trail had gone cold, I received a call from Eddie, telling me he'd received a call from Fredrik. I arranged to meet Eddie in a coffee shop in the piazza; the less we shared over the phone, the better. When we arrived, Eddie couldn't wait to tell me about their conversation.

"Fredrik must have been mulling over every scenario possible. He said that it may be nothing, but about three months ago a woman came into the shop and said that she was interested in buying rare antique jewellery." Eddie took a sip of his coffee, then continued. "So, Fredrik showed her some pieces he had in stock, but she asked if he had any jewellery which was much older; she said that she was looking for 16th-century pieces. Fredrik still had a few pieces put aside from the second hoard that we took over for him – a few rings – and he showed them to her.

Apparently, she showed quite an interest as to where he had obtained such a beautiful collection. Fredrik gave her a vague response, saying he'd got them from an old friend, many years ago."

When Eddie stopped for another gulp of coffee, I impatiently asked: "Well, what happened next?"

Eddie continued: "She bought two rings from him, for forty-thousand euros, and promised that she would come back sometime, just in case he came into possession of more jewellery of this calibre. But, he said, he never saw her again."

"Does he know her name?" I asked.

"No, but he has C.C.T.V. in the shop, and said that we are welcome to come and look at it. I thanked him and said that I will contact him as soon as I have run the information past you."

We decided to keep this information between the two of us.

Olivia had returned to England briefly, for a visit with friends and family, so it felt like the right time for Eddie and myself to return to Antwerp. I called Olivia to let her know.

"Hello, darling, how are you? Are you having a good time catching up on everyone's news?"

She laughed and replied: "Everyone sends their regards – and, of course, I wish you were here, too. What about you: what have you been up to?"

I didn't like lying to Olivia, but I wanted to protect her, so I simply replied: "I've been keeping myself busy and out of trouble. Darling, Fredrik called to ask if Eddie and I would like to join Hendrik's family at his funeral."

"I thought they would have already had the funeral; it's been weeks since his death!" Olivia said.

"Yes, I thought the same, but apparently they had to have a post-mortem, and his body has only just been released."

"Well, be careful, and let me know when you are back so I can book my return flight home."

"Home? Did you just call Italy your home?" I joked.

Happily, she replied: "Yes, I suppose I did."

*

The next day, we arrived at Fredrik's shop.

After the usual greetings, Fredrik closed the shop and signalled for us to go upstairs to his apartment, where he kept the recordings from the shop. We made ourselves comfortable and Fredrik made coffee, accompanied by an array of Belgian biscuits.

Once seated, Fredrik pressed play on the C.C.T.V. recording, which he had stopped at the appropriate day and time, for us to watch.

We watched, increasingly ashen, as the mystery woman walked into the shop. We turned toward each other.

"Well, I am damned!" I gasped.

This was followed by Eddie defending what we could both blatantly see: "It can't be her! It's just someone who looks like her."

"Eddie, that's fucking Gianna!" I shouted, before turning to our host. "Can I have this tape, Fredrik?"

"Yes, of course. I can see you obviously know this woman."

Eddie reluctantly answered: "Yes, Fredrik, we do."

The journey back was solemn. I was trying to piece together how Gianna knew so much. How did she know about our mission? Who was supplying her with information? Was she involved with the repercussions which followed? Was she willing to have people killed? So many questions and so few answers...

The next morning, Eddie and I met Marco, Aldo and Ernesto in

Marco's warehouse. I showed them the videotape Fredrik gave me, and looked eagerly to see if I could sense any signs of guilt in their faces, but to no avail.

Marco broke the silence: "From tonight, we follow her every move. We might need to search her house, too, for any evidence she might have on us. But, until we know what we are dealing with, we do nothing."

So, Aldo and Ernesto followed her every move, day and night, for the next two weeks, with no irregularities to report. Nada. She went to work, she came home, she stayed in, she visited her mother's house – usually with groceries – and she had coffee with her friends. We would meet up at the warehouse every other night for an update.

"Haven't you noticed any suspicious actions at all?" I asked.

Aldo looked at Ernesto and shrugged his shoulders, before saying: "Well, she is constantly looking over her shoulder, and I also noticed that she is a little bit rude when she is with company, using her phone constantly. Once, she looked like she was arguing with someone, then hung up and went back to chatting with her friends. Apart from this, we have nothing else to report to you."

"We have to step it up a bit; we need to search her house," I responded.

Marco jumped in, quickly: "Nathan, we need to make sure we are well prepared before we do such a thing. We don't want to get caught break into a poliziotti's house!"

So, again we waited patiently for a break.

Finally, we got a little luck on our side. Marco called me.

"Hello, cousin. Do you fancy a stroll to the countryside?"

Assuming this was leading to something, I replied: "I suppose so."

"Good. Get ready and I will pick you up in twenty minutes. Today's a good day for a picnic. Our friends are keeping an acquaintance of ours company, on a train heading for Florence."

"I'm assuming it's just me and you breaking into Gianna's place?"

"Yes, Nathan. I decided not to wait. With the realization that Gianna has been spying on us, I wouldn't be surprised if our phones or houses are bugged. Relax, it's not as if this is my first time entering a place illegally."

"I don't want to know," I replied.

Fortunately for us, Gianna lived in a semi-rural area. The

place was deserted.

We rang the doorbell, just in case, and when there was no answer, I kept watch whilst Marco picked the door lock. Within minutes we were inside.

We headed upstairs and took a bedroom each to search. Afterward, we met on the landing and both shook our heads, signalling that we had found nothing. Marco instructed me to search the ground floor, before heading to the outbuildings of the property. I was still searching for clues when Marco returned.

"I think I have found what we're looking for."

I followed Marco into the garage, and watched as he opened a rusty wine barrel. Inside was a large container containing handguns, ammunition, two automatic machine guns, surveillance equipment and videotape recordings.

We took the videotapes and the ammunition, making sure that none of the weapons were left loaded. Then, making sure we wiped away any evidence of our being there, we left.

My heart was beating fast as we fled. I had never broken into anywhere before and hoped I would never have to do it again.

"Won't she notice that the guns have no ammunition?" I asked.

"You have a lot to learn, cousin. I replaced the ammunition

with blanks, even filling the weapons with blanks, too."

"Where did you get the... Don't answer; I don't need to know."

We drove straight back to the warehouse and played the video recordings. To my surprise, one of the tapes showed me and Eddie working by the altar inside the church, and another of us rolling back the altar, climbing down into the crypt and bringing up boxes of jewels. Gianna must have had cameras inside the church. But, how would she know which churches to cover? And how did she know about the exchange in Luxembourg? There was only one way she could have so much information.

"She bugged us."

"Yes, Nathan. She has most probably bugged your house, Eddie's flat, my office and car showroom, and maybe even my house."

So, we started our search for bugs. And, sure enough, at Eddie's work we found bugs on the phones, under the table and even a camera in a plant, sitting atop a filing cabinet.

We then decided to continue our hunt for Gianna's deceptions by searching Marco's house. Once we ascertained his house was bug-free, we went over to Eddie's place. He was surprised to see us.

"We just popped in for a coffee," Marco said, while I signalled for Eddie not to talk. Marco then looked around, almost immediately finding and disconnecting a bug above the doorframe in Eddie's sitting room. Eddie sadly got the message: he, too, had been bugged.

We walked across the square to my place.

I immediately apologized to Olivia, for forgetting to pick up something for our dinner.

She huffed jokily and said: "I don't know! Must I do everything in this house?"

I kissed her and thanked her, waving to her as she picked up her purse and shopping bag. As soon as she left, the search began.

We found no less than three devices, including one over a picture frame hanging on the wall.

"Fucking bitch!" I cursed. "I think it's time to pay her a visit."

Aldo and Ernesto kept Gianna under surveillance throughout her whole trip to Florence, and as soon as she was back, they called to let us know.

"It's time to pay our lovely Gianna a visit," Marco confirmed, "and put our plan into action."

Eddie drove ahead on his own, and Marco and I followed; Aldo and Ernesto were already there, keeping watch. We stopped about fifty metres from Gianna's house, while Eddie drove straight up to her doorway.

Eddie knocked on the door and Gianna opened it.

"Hello, Gianna. I was just driving around and I couldn't resist stopping by, to see how you've been keeping."

"I'm glad you did," she smiled. "Come in. It's been a long time. Do you want coffee?"

"Yes, please, that would be nice."

"The last time I saw you, Eddie, you were going back to England," she reminisced, bitterly.

"Yes, and now I'm back. So much has happened since that time… but you already know that."

"What do you mean?" Gianna asked, puzzled.

"God, you are something else! You know precisely what I am talking about: four men badly wounded – one dead; guns and microphones; tapes and disguises! Gianna, the game is up; it's time to do some explaining."

In that moment, Gianna knew she had been rumbled.

Before she could utter a word, there was a knock on the door.

Eddie stood up. "Let me open the door for you."

As he did so, in walked me and Marco.

Looking over at her, I echoed what Eddie had just said: "As your ex-boyfriend just stated, Gianna, we would *all* like to hear your explanation."

Now scared and close to tears, Gianna started to explain. She began by telling us that it all began when she paid her uncle a visit.

"What's your uncle got to do with all this?" I asked.

"My uncle Lorenzo is the blacksmith that you paid a visit. He told me a story about two men, supposedly Vatican agents, looking for lost treasure. The agents told him that the treasure was stored in churches for safekeeping. He was struggling with the next part of his story, but I encouraged him to continue: he was very apologetic for stealing from the church, and for not reporting his discovery to the local authorities; he felt better for handing over what he had taken. I asked him to describe the men who had called on him, and his description sounded just like two Englishmen I knew! At first, I didn't believe you two were capable of pulling off such a ruse; how wrong I was! A few weeks later, my uncle was dead, supposedly by a hit-and-run driver; I believe he was murdered because he knew too much.

"A few days later, I was driving past the church of San Biagio, when I saw two men enter the church. I parked the car in the piazza and walked over; the door was open, so I let myself in and hid behind the marble pillar. I saw the two men in the front of the altar: it was you two, Eddie and Nathan. Then, some people entered the church and one of you told them that it was closed for major renovations, then as soon as the people left Eddie locked the door. I watched you both, looking around the church as if you were searching for something; I was puzzled and curious. I could then hear knocking and tapping sounds echoing around the church, but you were by now out of my view, so I could not see what you were doing. Then I remembered Father Luca telling me how God works in mysterious ways, and that two kind strangers wanted to restore San Biagio Church." Gianna took a moment, then continued: "What with the information given to me by my uncle, his sudden accident and Father Luca's revelation, I knew that you two were up to something. When you both left the church that day, you locked me inside, but I managed to get out, through an open window. But, wanting to know what you were up to, I came back the same evening with a friend, and we set up a hidden camera, by the statue of the Holy Mary.

"It took two days for you to come back. But then, caught on

film, I saw you roll back the altar and enter the vault. And when you came up you were carrying treasure, which must have been hidden there for centuries! I wanted to know just how you knew there would be something hidden in this church, and what exactly it was that you found. Were there other churches? And how valuable was the total pot worth? So, I bugged you. The rest you know."

As she finished her confession, we all looked at her, wondering how this was going to end.

I looked Gianna straight in the eyes and asked her who else knew about what she had just confessed, other than her wounded friends.

She was adamant that nobody knew the full story. Even her friends were not interested in the details; they were just paid to set up an ambush and leave.

"You mean they are not part of the Italian authorities, too?" I asked.

"No, I swear to you. This was personal to me; I wanted answers."

Gianna took a deep breath, before continuing: "So, now what? What are you going to do with me?"

I stepped outside with Marco, to discuss what to do next.

Marco didn't like loose ends and wanted Gianna silenced. I, on the other hand, was an ordinary man, wanting no more than to at long last settle down with the woman I loved, and not draw any more unnecessary attention my way.

"Marco, this all began with you calling me to let me know that old Agostino had passed away; if it wasn't for me buying the old man's property, we wouldn't be having this conversation today. My gut feeling is telling me that his death was not of natural causes, and I would like to think that, in some ways, what we have uncovered means that his death was not in vain. Marco, we have uncovered a conspiracy that could rewrite history, and so much good has already been achieved with the proceeds. I know I can't stop you from doing what you will, but I want nothing to do with any more blood on my hands."

With that, I walked back into the room and looked at Eddie. "Come on, mate; it's time for us to leave."

I could see by the expression on his face that he was struggling with his emotions. I walked toward him and, putting a firm hand on his shoulder, we walked out of the house, toward the car.

Before opening the car doors, we heard a loud bang.

We stopped in our tracks and turned toward Gianna's front

door. Marco was walking slowly toward us. We were horrified.

"She's okay," Eddie assured us; "I couldn't do it."

I looked at Eddie, and saw his huge smile spread.

"You'd better go back and see her, then," I said.

About the Author

Growing up in London, influenced heavily by my Italian mother, gave me a fascination with art and history, and a love of travel. From a very young age, we would go by train to visit the family my mother had left behind. History has always been of interest to me, and holidays were more to me than sitting on a beach; they were a chance to immerse myself in learning from people of different backgrounds. In particular, I enjoyed watching craftsmen restoring bits and pieces from old to new; it comes as no surprise that I became a draughtsman.

The house in *1537 Conspiracy* is real, and one I had the privilege to restore, as are the frescos, the tabernacle and other features mentioned. The book is based on many a night lying on a camper bed, letting my imagination loose, and wondering what if the walls in this remarkable house could speak…

Acknowledgements

The publisher would like to thank Russell Spencer, Matt Vidler, Laura-Jayne Humphrey, Lianne Bailey-Woodward, Leonard West and Susan Woodard for their hard work and efforts in bringing this book to publication.

About the Publisher

L.R. Price Publications is dedicated to publishing books by unknown authors.

We use a mixture of both traditional and modern publishing options, to bring our authors' words to the wider world.

We print, publish, distribute and market books in a variety of formats including paper and hardback, electronic books, digital audiobooks and online.

If you are an author interested in getting your book published, or a book retailer interested in selling our books, please contact us.

www.lrpricepublications.com

L.R. Price Publications Ltd,
27 Old Gloucester Street,
London, WC1N 3AX.
020 3051 9572
publishing@lrprice.com

Printed in Great Britain
by Amazon

24795059R00195